"I'm fully aware our impending marriage has its base in mutual convenience," Aysha stated.

"But," she continued, "I insist on your fidelity."

Carlo's eyes narrowed and became chillingly calm. "My fidelity isn't in question."

"Isn't it? In this marriage, there's room for two of us. There's no way I'll turn a blind eye to you having a mistress on the side!"

Harlequin Presents® invites you to see how the other half marries in:

SOCIETY WEDDINGS

*They're gorgeous, they're glamorous...
and they're getting married!*

Throughout this sensational miniseries you've been our VIP guest at some of the most talked-about weddings of the decade—spectacular events where the cream of society gather to celebrate the marriages of dazzling brides and grooms in equally breathtaking, international locations.

At each lavish ceremony we've met some extraspecial men and women—all rich, royal or just renowned! We now reach the climax of this series with Helen Bianchin's **A Convenient Bridegroom.** So turn the pages and enter a sophisticated world of wealth and glamor—where there's no end of scandal, surprises...and passion!

HELEN BIANCHIN

A Convenient Bridegroom

SOCIETY **W**EDDINGS

HARLEQUIN®

TORONTO • NEW YORK • LONDON
AMSTERDAM • PARIS • SYDNEY • HAMBURG
STOCKHOLM • ATHENS • TOKYO • MILAN • MADRID
PRAGUE • WARSAW • BUDAPEST • AUCKLAND

ISBN 0-373-12067-2

A CONVENIENT BRIDEGROOM

First North American Publication 1999.

Copyright © 1999 by Helen Bianchin.

This edition published by arrangement with Harlequin Books S.A.

® and TM are trademarks of the publisher. Trademarks indicated with ® are registered in the United States Patent and Trademark Office, the Canadian Trade Marks Office and in other countries.

Visit us at www.romance.net

Printed in U.S.A.

CHAPTER ONE

'NIGHT, *cara*. You will be staying over, won't you?'

Subtle, very subtle, Aysha conceded. It never ceased to amaze that her mother could state a command in the form of a suggestion, and phrase it as a question. As if Aysha had a choice.

For as long as she could remember, her life had been stage-managed. The most exclusive of private schools, extra-curricular private tuition. Holidays abroad, winter resorts. Ballet, riding school, languages...she spoke fluent Italian and French.

Aysha Benini was a product of her parents' upbringing. Fashioned, styled and presented as a visual attestation to family wealth and status.

Something which must be upheld at any cost.

Even her chosen career as an interior decorator added to the overall image.

'Darling?'

Aysha crossed the room and brushed her lips to her mother's cheek. 'Probably.'

Teresa Benini allowed one eyebrow to form an elegant arch. 'Your father and I won't expect you home.'

Case closed. Aysha checked her evening purse, selected her car key, and turned towards the door. 'See you later.'

'Have a good time.'

5

What did Teresa Benini consider a *good time*? An exquisitely served meal eaten in a trendy restaurant with Carlo Santangelo, followed by a long night of loving in Carlo's bed?

Aysha slid in behind the wheel of her black Porsche Carrera, fired the engine, then eased the car down the driveway, cleared the electronic gates, and traversed the quiet tree-lined street towards the main arterial road leading from suburban Vaucluse into the city.

A shaft of sunlight caught the diamond-studded gold band with its magnificent solitaire on the third finger of her left hand. Brilliantly designed, horrendously expensive, it was a befitting symbol representing the intended union of Giuseppe Benini's daughter to Luigi Santangelo's son.

Benini-Santangelo, Aysha mused as she joined the flow of city-bound traffic.

Two immigrants from two neighbouring properties in a northern Italian town had travelled in their late teens to Sydney, where they'd worked two jobs every day of the week, saved every cent, and set up a cement business in their mid-twenties.

Forty years on, Benini-Santangelo was a major name in Sydney's building industry, with a huge plant and a fleet of concrete tankers.

Each man had married a suitable wife, sadly produced only one child apiece; they lived in fine homes, drove expensive cars, and had given their children the best education that money could buy.

Both families had interacted closely on a social and personal level for as long as Aysha could remember. The bond between them was strong, more than friends. Almost family.

The New South Head Road wound down towards Rose Bay, and Aysha took a moment to admire the view.

At six-thirty on a fine late summer's evening the ocean resembled a sapphire jewel, merging with a sky clear of cloud or pollution. Prime real estate overlooked numerous coves and bays where various sailing craft lay anchored. Tall city buildings rose in differing architectural design, structured towers of glass and steel, providing a splendid backdrop to the Opera House and the wide span of the Harbour Bridge.

Traffic became more dense as she drew close to the city, and there were the inevitable delays at computer-controlled intersections.

Consequently it was almost seven when she drew into the curved entrance of the hotel and consigned her car to valet parking.

She could, *should* have allowed Carlo to collect her, or at least driven to his apartment. It would have been more practical, sensible.

Except tonight she didn't feel *sensible*.

Aysha nodded to the concierge as she entered the lobby, and she hadn't taken more than three steps towards the bank of sofas and single chairs when a familiar male frame rose to full height and moved forward to greet her.

Carlo Santangelo.

Just the sight of him was enough to send her heart racing to a quickened beat. Her breath caught in her throat, and she forced herself to monitor the rise and fall of her chest.

In his late thirties, he stood three inches over six feet and possessed the broad shoulders and hard-muscled body of a man who coveted physical fitness. Sculpted raw-boned facial features highlighted planes and angles, accenting a powerful jaw, strong chin, and a sensuously moulded mouth. Well-cut thick dark brown hair was stylishly groomed, and his eyes were incredibly dark, almost black.

Aysha had no recollection of witnessing his temper. Yet there could be no doubt he possessed one, for his eyes could darken to obsidian, the mouth thin, and his voice assume the chill of an ice floe.

'Aysha.' He leant down and brushed his mouth against her own, lingered, then he lifted his head and caught both of her hands in his.

Dear God, he was something. The clean male smell of him teased her nostrils, combining with his subtle aftershave.

Her stomach executed a series of somersaults, and her pulse hammered heavily enough to be almost audible. Did she affect him the way he affected her?

Doubtful, she conceded, aware of precisely where she fitted in the scheme of things. Bianca had been his first love, the beautiful young girl he'd married ten years ago, only to lose her in a fatal car accident mere weeks after the honeymoon. Aysha had cried silent tears at the wedding, and wept openly at Bianca's funeral.

Afterwards he'd flung himself into work, earning

a reputation in the business arena as a superb strategist, able to negotiate with enviable skill.

He had dated many women, and selectively taken what they offered without thought of replacing the beautiful young girl who had all too briefly shared his name.

Until last year, when he'd focused his attention on Aysha, strengthening the affectionate bond between them into something much more personal, more intimate.

His proposal of marriage had overwhelmed her, for Carlo had been the object of her affection for as long as she could remember, and she could pinpoint the moment when teenage hero-worship had changed and deepened into love.

A one-sided love, for she was under no illusion. The marriage would strengthen the Benini-Santangelo conglomerate and forge it into another generation.

'Hungry?'

At the sound of Carlo's drawled query Aysha offered a winsome smile, and her eyes assumed a teasing sparkle. 'Starving.'

'Then let's go eat, shall we?' Carlo placed an arm round her waist and led her towards a bank of elevators.

The top of her head came level with his shoulder, and her slender frame held a fragility that was in direct contrast to strength of mind and body.

She could, he reflected musingly as he depressed the call button, have turned into a terrible brat. Yet for all the pampering, by an indulgent but fiercely protective mother, Aysha was without guile. Nor did she have an inflated sense of her own importance. Instead, she was a warm, intelligent, witty and very attractive young woman whose smile transformed her features into something quite beautiful.

The restaurant was situated on a high floor offering magnificent views of the city and harbour. Expensive, exclusive, and a personal favourite, for the chef was a true artiste with an expertise and flair that had earned him fame and fortune in several European countries.

The lift doors slid open, and she preceded Carlo into the cubicle, then stood in silence as they were transported with electronic speed.

'That bad, hmm?'

Aysha cast him a quick glance, saw the musing cynicism apparent, and didn't know whether to be amused or resigned that he'd divined her silence and successfully attributed it to a ghastly day.

Was she that transparent? Somehow she didn't think so. At least not with most people. However, Carlo was an entity all on his own, and she'd accepted a long time ago that there was very little she could manage to keep hidden from him.

'Where would you like me to begin?' She wrinkled her nose at him, then she lifted a hand and proceeded to tick off each finger in turn. 'An irate client, an even more irate floor manager, imported fabric caught up in a wharf strike, or the dress fitting from hell?' She rolled her eyes. 'Choose.'

The elevator slid to a halt, and she walked at his side to the restaurant foyer.

'Signor Santangelo, Signorina Benini. Welcome.' The maître d' greeted them with a fulsome smile, and accorded them the deference of valued patrons. He didn't even suggest a table, merely led them to the one they preferred, adjacent the floor-to-ceiling window.

There was, Aysha conceded, a certain advantage in being socially well placed. It afforded impeccable service.

The wine steward appeared the instant they were seated, and Aysha deferred to Carlo's choice of white wine.

'Iced water, please,' she added, then watched as Carlo leaned back in his chair to regard her with interest.

'How is Teresa?'

'Now there's a leading question, if ever there was one,' Aysha declared lightly. 'Perhaps you could be more specific?'

'She's driving you insane.' His faint drawling tones caused the edges of her mouth to tilt upwards in a semblance of wry humour.

'You're good. Very good,' she acknowledged with cynical approval.

One eyebrow rose, and there was gleaming amusement evident. 'Shall I try for excellent and guess the current crisis?' he ventured. 'Or are you going to tell me?'

'The wedding dress.' Visualising the scene earlier in the day brought a return of tension as she vividly recalled Teresa's calculated insistence and the seamstress's restrained politeness. Dammit, it should be so easy. They'd agreed on the style, the material. The fit was perfect. Yet Teresa hadn't been able to leave it alone.

'Problems?' He had no doubt there would be many, most of which would be of Teresa's making.

'The dressmaker is not appreciative of Mother's interference with the design.' Aysha experienced momentary remorse, for the gown was truly beautiful, a vision of silk, satin and lace.

'I see.'

'No,' she corrected. 'You don't.' She paused as the wine steward delivered the wine, and went through the tasting ritual with Carlo, before retreating.

'What don't I see, *cara*?' Carlo queried lightly. 'That Teresa, like most Italian *mammas*, wants the perfect wedding for her daughter. The perfect venue, caterers, food, wine, *bomboniera*, the cake, limousines. And the dress must be outstanding.'

'You've forgotten the flowers,' Aysha reminded him mildly. 'The florist is at the end of his tether. The caterer is ready to quit because he says *his* tiramisu is an art form and he will not, *not*, you understand, use my grandmother's recipe from the Old Country.'

Carlo's mouth formed a humorous twist. 'Teresa is a superb cook,' he complimented blandly.

Teresa was superb at everything; that was the trouble. Consequently, she expected others to be equally superb. The *trouble* as such, was that while Teresa Benini enjoyed the prestige of employing the *best* money could buy, she felt bound to check every little detail to ensure it came up to her impossibly high standard.

Retaining household staff had always been a problem for as long as Aysha could remember. They came and left with disturbing rapidity due to her mother's refusal to delegate even the most minor of chores.

The waiter arrived with the menu, and because he was new, and very young, they listened in silence as he explained the intricacies of each dish, gave his considered recommendations, then very solicitously noted their order before retreating with due deference to relay it to the kitchen.

Aysha lifted her glass and took a sip of chilled water, then regarded the man seated opposite over the rim of the stemmed goblet.

'How seriously would you consider an elopement?'

Carlo swirled the wine in his goblet, then lifted it to his lips and savoured the delicate full-bodied flavour.

'Is there any particular reason why you'd want to incur Teresa's wrath by wrecking the social event of the year?'

'It would never do,' she agreed solemnly. 'Although I'm almost inclined to plug for sanity and suffer the wrath.'

One eyebrow slanted, and his dark eyes assumed a quizzical gleam.

The waiter delivered their starters; minestrone and a superb linguini with seafood sauce.

'Two weeks, *cara*,' Carlo reminded her.

It was a lifetime. One she wasn't sure she'd survive intact.

She should have moved out of home into an apartment of her own. Would have, if Teresa hadn't dismissed the idea as ridiculous when she had a wing in the house all to herself, complete with gym, sauna and entertainment lounge. She had her own car, her own garage, and technically she could come and go as she pleased.

Aysha picked up her fork, deftly wound on a portion of pasta and savoured it. Ambrosia. The sauce was *perfecto*.

'Good?'

She wound on another portion and held it to his lips. 'Try some.' She hadn't intended it to be an intimate gesture, and her eyes flared slightly as he placed his fingers over hers, guided the fork, and then held her gaze as he slid the pasta into his mouth.

Her stomach jolted, then settled, and she was willing to swear she could hear her own heartbeat thudding in her ears.

He didn't even have to try, and she became caught up with the alchemy that was his alone.

A warm smile curved his lips as he dipped a spoon into his minestrone and lifted it invitingly towards her own. 'Want to try mine?'

She took a small mouthful, then shook her head when he offered her another. Did he realise just how difficult it was for her to retain a measure of sangfroid at moments like these?

'We have a rehearsal at the church tomorrow evening,' Carlo reminded her, and saw her eyes darken.

Aysha replaced her fork, her appetite temporarily diminished. 'Six-thirty,' she concurred evenly. 'After which the wedding party dine together.'

Both sets of parents, the bride and groom to-be, the bridesmaids and their attendants, the flower girls and page boys and *their* parents.

Followed the next day by a bridal shower. Hardly a casual affair, with just very close friends, a few nibblies and champagne. The guest list numbered fifty, it was being catered, and Teresa had arranged entertainment.

To add to her stress levels, she'd stubbornly refused to begin six weeks' leave of absence from work until a fortnight before the wedding.

On the positive side, it kept her busy, her mind occupied, and minimised the growing tension with her mother. The negative was hours early morning and evening spent at the breathtaking harbourside mansion Carlo had built, overseeing installation of carpets, drapes, selecting furniture, co-ordinating colours. And doing battle with Teresa when their tastes didn't match and Teresa overstretched her advisory capacity. Something which happened fairly frequently.

'Penny for them.'

Aysha glanced across the table and caught Carlo's teasing smile.

'I was thinking about the house.' That much was true. 'It's all coming together very well.'

'You're happy with it?'

'How could I not be?' she countered simply, visualising the modern architectural design with its five sound-proofed self-contained wings converging onto a central courtyard. The interior was designed for light and space, with a suspended art gallery, a small theatre and games room. A sunken area featured spa and sauna, and a jet pool.

It was a showcase, a place to entertain guests and business associates. Aysha planned to make it a home.

The wine waiter appeared and refilled each goblet, followed closely by the young waiter, who removed their plates prior to serving the main course.

Carlo ate with the enjoyment of a man who consumed nourishment wisely but well, his use of cutlery decisive.

He was the consummate male, sophisticated, dynamic, and possessed of a primitive sensuality that drew women to him like a magnet. Men envied his ruthlessness and charm, and knew the combination to be lethal.

Aysha recognised each and every one of his qualities, and wondered if she was woman enough to hold him.

'Would you care to order dessert, Miss Benini?'

The young waiter's desire to please was almost embarrassing, and she offered him a gentle smile. 'No, thanks, I'll settle for coffee.'

'You've made a conquest,' Carlo drawled as the waiter retreated from their table.

Her eyes danced with latent mischief. 'Ah, you say the nicest things.'

'Should I appear jealous, do you think?'

She wanted to say, *only if you are*. And since that was unlikely, it became easy to play the game.

'Well, he *is* young, and good-looking.' She pretended to consider. 'Probably a university student working nights to pay for his education. Which would indicate he has potential.' She held Carlo's dark gleaming gaze and offered him a brilliant smile. 'Do you think he'd give up the room he probably rents, sell his wheels...a Vespa scooter at a guess...and be a kept toy-boy?'

His soft laughter sent shivers over the surface of her skin, raising fine body hairs as all her nerve-endings went haywire.

'I think I should take you home.'

'I came in my own car, remember?' she reminded him, and saw his eyes darken, the gleam intensify.

'A bid for independence, or an indication you're not going to share my bed tonight?'

She summoned a winsome smile, and her eyes shone with wicked humour. 'Teresa is of the opinion catering to your physical needs should definitely be my priority.'

'And Teresa knows best?' His voice was silky-smooth, and she wasn't deceived for a second.

'My mother believes in covering all the bases,' Aysha relayed lightly.

His gaze didn't shift, and she was almost willing to swear he could read her mind. 'As you do?'

Her expression sobered. 'I don't have a hidden agenda.' Did he know she was in love with him? Had loved him for as long as she could remember? She hoped not, for it would afford him an unfair advantage.

'Finish your coffee,' Carlo bade gently. 'Then we'll leave.' He lifted a hand in silent summons, and the waiter appeared with the bill.

Aysha watched as Carlo signed the slip and added a generous tip, then he leaned back in his chair and surveyed her thoughtfully.

She was tense, but covered it well. His eyes narrowed faintly. 'Do we have anything planned next weekend?'

'Mother has something scheduled for every day until the wedding,' she declared with unaccustomed cynicism.

'Have Teresa reorganise her diary.'

Aysha looked at him with interest. 'And if she won't?'

'Tell her I've surprised you with airline tickets and accommodation for a weekend on the Gold Coast.'

'Have you?'

His smile held humour. 'I'll make the call the minute we reach my apartment.'

Her eyes shone, and she broke into light laughter. 'My knight in shining armour.'

Carlo's voice was low, husky, and held amusement. 'Escape,' he accorded. 'Albeit brief.' He stood to his feet and reached out a hand to take hold of hers. His gleaming gaze seared right through to her heart. 'You can thank me later.'

Together they made their way through the room to the front desk.

The maître d' was courteously solicitous. 'I'll arrange with the concierge to have your cars brought to the front entrance.'

Both vehicles were waiting when they reached the lobby. Carlo saw her seated behind the wheel of her Porsche, then he crossed to his Mercedes to fire the engine within seconds and ease into the line of traffic.

Aysha followed, sticking close behind him as he traversed the inner city streets heading east towards Rose Bay and his penthouse apartment.

When they reached it she drove down into the underground car park, took the space adjoining his private bay, then walked at his side towards the bank of lifts in companionable silence.

They didn't *need* a house, she determined minutes later as she stepped into the plush apartment lobby.

The drapes weren't drawn, and the view out over the harbour was magnificent. Fairy lights, she mused as she crossed the lounge to the floor-to-ceiling glass stretching across one entire wall.

City buildings, street lights, brightly coloured neon vying with tall concrete spires and an indigo sky.

Aysha heard him pick up the phone, followed by the sound of his voice as he arranged flights and accommodation for the following weekend.

'We could have easily lived here,' she murmured as he came to stand behind her.

'So we could.' He put his arms around her waist and pulled her back against him.

She felt his chin rest on the top of her head, sensed the warmth of his breath as it teased her hair, and was unable to prevent the slight shiver as his lips sought the vulnerable hollow beneath the lobe of one ear.

She almost closed her eyes and pretended it was real. That *love* not lust, and *need* not want, was Carlo's motivation.

A silent groan rose and died in her throat as his mouth travelled to the edge of her neck and nuzzled, his tongue, his lips erotic instruments as he tantalised the rapidly beating pulse.

His hands moved, one to her breast as he sought a sensitive peak, while the other splayed low over her stomach.

She wanted to urge him to quicken the pace, to dispense with her clothes while she feverishly tore every barrier from his body until there was nothing between them.

She wanted to be lifted high in his arms and sink down onto him, then clutch hold of him as he took her for the ride of her life.

Everything about him was too controlled. Even in bed he never lost that control completely, as she did.

There were times when she wanted to cry out that while she could accept Bianca as an important part of his past, *she* was his future. Except she never said the words. Perhaps because she was afraid of his response.

Now she turned in his arms and reached for him, her mouth seeking his as she gave herself up completely to the heat of passion.

He caught her urgency and effortlessly swept her into his arms and carried her into the bedroom.

Aysha's fingers worked on his shirt buttons, unfastened the buckle on his belt, then pulled his shirt free.

His nipples were hard, and she savoured each one in turn, then used her teeth to tease, aware that Carlo had deftly removed most of her clothes.

She heard his intake of breath seconds ahead of the soft thud as he discarded one shoe and the other, then dispensed with his trousers.

'Wait.' His voice was low and slightly husky, and she ran her hands over his ribcage, searched the hard plane of his stomach and reached for him.

'So you want to play, hmm?'

CHAPTER TWO

CARLO caught hold of her arms and let his hands slide up to cup her shoulders as he buried his mouth in the vulnerable hollow at the edge of her neck.

Her subtle perfume teased his senses, and he nuzzled the sensitive skin, tasted it, nipped ever so gently with his teeth, and felt the slight spasm of her body's reaction to his touch.

She was a generous lover. Passionate, with a sense of adventure and fun he found endearing.

He trailed his lips down the slope of her breast and suckled one tender peak, savoured, then moved to render a similar supplication to its twin.

Did he know what he did to her? Aysha felt a stab of pain at the thought that his lovemaking might be contrived. A practised set of moves that pushed all the right buttons.

Once, just once she wanted to feel the tremors of need shake his body…for her, only her. To know that she could make him so crazy with desire that he had no restraint.

Was it asking too much to want *love*? She wore his ring. Soon *she* would bear his name. It should be enough.

She wanted to mean so much more to him than just a satisfactory bed partner, a charming hostess.

Take what he's prepared to give, and be grateful,

a tiny voice prompted. *A cup half-full is better than one that is empty.*

Her hands linked at his nape and she drew his head down to hers, exulting in the feel of his mouth as he shaped her own.

She let her tongue slide against his, then conducted a slow, sweeping circle before initiating a probing dance that was almost as evocative as the sexual act itself.

His hand shaped her nape and held fast her head, while the other slipped low over one hip, cupped her bottom and drew her close in against him.

She wanted him *now*, hard and fast, without any preliminaries. To be able to feel the power, the strength, without caution or care. As if he couldn't bear to wait a second longer to effect possession.

The familiar slide of his fingers, the gentle probing exploration as he sought the warm moistness of her feminine core brought a gasping sigh from her lips.

Followed by a despairing groan as he began an evocative stimulation. It wasn't fair that he should have such intimate knowledge and be aware precisely how to wield it to drive a woman wild.

His mouth hardened, and his jaw took control of hers, moving it in rhythm with his own.

She clutched hold of his shoulders and held on as his fingers probed deeper, and just as she thought she could bear it no longer he shifted position.

A cry rose and died in her throat as he slid into her in one long, thrusting movement.

Dear God, that felt good. So good. She murmured

her pleasure, then gave a startled gasp as he tumbled her down onto the bed and withdrew.

His mouth left hers, and began a seeking trail down her throat, tasting the vulnerable hollows at the base of her neck, the soft, quivering flesh of each breast, the indentation of her navel.

She knew his intention, and felt the flame lick along every nerve-end, consuming every sensitised nerve-cell until she was close to conflagration.

Her head tossed from one side to the other as sensation took hold of her whole body. Part of her wanted to tell him to stop before it became unbearable, but the husky admonition sounded so low in her throat as to be indistinguishable.

He was skilled, so very highly skilled in giving a woman pleasure. The slight graze of his teeth, the erotic laving of his tongue. He knew just where to touch to urge her towards the edge. And how to hold her there, until she begged for release.

Aysha thought she cried out, and she bit down hard as Carlo feathered light kisses over her quivering stomach, then paused to suckle at her breast,

His mouth closed on hers, and she arched up against him as he entered her in one surging movement, stretching delicate tissues to their utmost capacity.

He began to move, slowly at first, then with increasing depth and strength as she became consumed with the feel of him.

His skin, her own, was warm and slick with sweat, and the blood ran through her veins like quicksilver.

It was more than a physical joining, for she gifted

him her heart, her soul, everything. She was *his*. Only his. At that moment she would have died for him, so complete was her involvement.

Frightening, shattering, she reflected a long time later as she lay curled into the warmth of his body. For it almost destroyed her concept of who and what she had become beneath his tutelage.

The steady rise and fall of his chest was reassuring, the beat of his heart strong. The lazy stroke of his fingers along her spine indicated he wasn't asleep yet, and the slight pressure against the indentations of each vertebrae was soothing. She could feel his lips brush lightly over her hair as she drifted into a peaceful sleep.

It was the soft, hazy aftermath of great lovemaking. A time for whispered avowals of love, Aysha thought as she woke, the affirmation of commitment.

Aysha wanted to utter the words, and hear them in return. Yet she knew she would die a silent death if he didn't respond in kind. She pressed a light butterfly kiss to the muscled ridge of his chest and traced a gentle circle with the tip of her tongue.

He tasted of musk, edged with a faint tang that was wholly male. She nipped the hard flesh with her teeth and bestowed a love-bite, then she soothed it gently before moving close to a sensitive male nipple.

She trailed her fingers over one hip, lingered near his groin, and felt his stomach muscles tense.

'That could prove dangerous,' Carlo warned as she began to caress him with gentle intimacy.

The soft slide of one finger, as fleeting as the tip of a butterfly's wing, in a careful tactile exploration. Incredible how the male organ could engorge and enlarge in size. Almost frightening, its degree of power as instrument to a woman's pleasure.

Aysha had the desire to tantalise him to the brink of madness, and unleash everything that was wild and untamed, until there were no boundaries. Just two people as one, attuned and in perfect accord on every level. Spiritual, mental and physical.

A gasp escaped her throat as he clasped both hands on her waist and swept her to sit astride him.

Excitement spiralled through her body as he arched his hips and sent her tumbling down against his chest.

One hand slid to her nape as he angled her head to his, then his mouth was on hers, all heat and passion as he took possession.

The kiss seared her heart, branding her in a way that made her *his*...totally. Mind, body, and soul. She had no thought for anything but the man and the storm raging within.

It made anything she'd shared before seem less. Dear Lord, she'd ached for his passion. But this...this was raw, primitive. Mesmeric. Ravaging.

She met and matched his movements, driven by a hunger so intense she had no recollection of time or place.

Aysha wasn't even aware when he reversed positions, and it was the gentling of his touch, the gradual loss of intensity that intruded on her conscious mind and brought with it a slow return to sanity.

There was a sense of exquisite wonderment, a sensation of wanting desperately to hold onto the moment in case it might fracture and fragment.

She didn't feel the soft warmth of tears as they slid slowly down her cheeks. Nor was she aware of the sexual heat emanating from her skin, or the slight trembling of her body as Carlo used his hands, his lips to bring her down.

He absorbed the dampness on one cheek, then pressed his lips against one closed eyelid, before moving to effect a similar supplication on the other. His hands shifted as he gently rolled onto his back, carrying her with him so she lay cradled against the length of his body.

Slight tremors shook her slim form, and he brought her mouth to his in a soft, evocative joining. His fingers trailed the shape of her, gently exploring the slim supple curves, the slender waist, the soft curve of her buttocks.

It was Carlo who broke contact long minutes later, and she trailed a hand down the edge of his cheek.

'I get first take on the shower. You make the coffee,' she whispered.

His slow smile caused havoc with her pulse-rate. 'We share the shower, then I'll organise coffee while you cook breakfast.'

'Chauvinist,' Aysha commented with musing tolerance.

His lips caressed her breast, and desire arrowed through her body, hot, needy, and wildly wanton. 'We can always miss breakfast and focus on the shower.'

His arousal was a potent force, and her eyes danced with mischief as she contemplated the option. 'As much as the offer attracts me, I need *food* to charge my energy levels.' She placed the tip of a finger over his lips, then gave a mild yelp as he nipped it with his teeth. 'That calls for revenge.'

Carlo's hands spanned her waist and he shifted her to one side, then he leaned over her. 'Try it.'

She rose to the challenge at once, although the balance of power soon became uneven, and then it hardly seemed to matter any more who won or lost.

Afterwards she had the quickest shower on record, then she dressed, swept her hair into a twist at her nape, added blusher, eye colour and mascara.

She looked, Carlo noted with respect, as if she'd spent thirty minutes on her grooming instead of the five it had taken her.

'Sit down and eat,' he commanded as he slid an omelette onto a plate. 'Coffee's ready.'

'You're a gem among men,' Aysha complimented as she sipped the coffee. Pure nectar on the palate, and the omelette was perfection.

'From chauvinist to gem in the passage of twenty minutes,' he drawled with unruffled ease, and she spared him a wicked grin in between mouthfuls.

'Don't get a swelled head.'

She watched as he poured himself some coffee then joined her at the table. The dark navy towelling robe accented his breadth of shoulder, and dark curling hair showed at the vee of the lapels. Her eyes slid down to the belt tied at his waist, and lingered.

'You don't have time to find out,' he mocked lazily, and she offered a stunning smile.

'It's my last day at work.' She rose to her feet and gulped the last mouthful of coffee. 'But as of tomorrow…'

'Promises,' Carlo taunted, and she reached up to brush her lips to his cheek, except he moved his head and they touched his mouth instead.

'Got to rush,' she said with genuine regret. 'See you tonight.'

Her job was important to her, and she loved the concept of using colour and design to make a house a home. The right furnishings, furniture, fittings, so that it all added up to a beautiful whole that was both eye-catching and comfortable. She'd earned a reputation for going that extra mile for a client, exploring every avenue in the search to get it right.

However, there were days when phone calls didn't produce the results she wanted, and today was one of them. Added to which she had to run a final check over all the orders that were due to come in while she was away. An awesome task, just on its own.

Then there was lunch with some of her fellow staff, and the presentation of a wedding gift…an exquisite crystal platter. The afternoon seemed to fly on wings, and it was after six when she rode the lift to Carlo's penthouse.

'Ten minutes,' she promised him as she entered the lounge, and she stepped out of heeled pumps *en route* to the shower.

Aysha was ready in nine, and he snagged her arm as she raced towards the door.

'Slow down,' he directed, and she threw him an urgent glance.

'We're late. We should have left already.' She tugged her hand and made no impression. 'They'll be waiting for us.'

He pulled her close, and lowered his head down to hers. 'So they'll wait a little longer.'

His mouth touched hers with such incredible gentleness her insides began to melt, and she gave a faint despairing groan as her lips parted beneath the pressure of his.

Minutes later he lifted his head and surveyed the languid expression softening those beautiful smoky grey eyes. Better, he noted silently. Some of the tension had ebbed away, and she looked slightly more relaxed.

'OK, let's go.'

'That was deliberate,' Aysha said a trifle ruefully as they rode the lift down to the underground car park, and caught his musing smile.

'Guilty.'

He'd slowed her galloping pace down to a relaxed trot, and she offered a smile in silent thanks as they left the lift and crossed to the Mercedes.

'How was your day?' she queried as she slid into the passenger seat and fastened her belt.

'Assembling quotes, checking computer print-outs, checking a building site. Numerous phone calls.'

'All hands-on stuff, huh?'

The large car sprang into instant life the moment he turned the key, and he spared her a wry smile as they gained street level.

'That about encapsulates it.'

The church was a beautiful old stone building set back from the road among well-tended lawns and gardens. Symmetrically planted trees and their spreading branches added to the portrayed seclusion.

There was an air of peace and grace apparent, meshing with the mystique of blessed holy ground.

Aysha drew a deep breath as she saw the several cars lining the curved driveway. Everyone was here.

Attending someone else's wedding, watching the ceremony on film or television, was a bit different from participating in one's own, albeit this was merely a rehearsal of the real thing.

'I want to carry the basket,' Emily, the youngest flower girl, insisted, and tried to wrest it from Samantha's grasp.

'I don't want to hold a pillow. It looks sissy,' Jonathon, the eldest page boy declared.

Oh, my. If he thought carrying a small satin lace-edged pillow demeaned his boyhood, then just wait until he had to get dressed in a miniature suit, satin waistcoat, buttoned shirt and bow-tie.

'Sissy,' the youngest page boy endorsed.

'You have to,' Emily insisted importantly.

'Don't.'

'Do so.'

Aysha didn't know whether to laugh or cry. 'What if Samantha carries the basket of rose petals, and Emily carries the pillow?'

It was almost possible to see the ensuing mental tussle as each little girl weighed the importance of each task.

'I want the pillow,' Samantha decided. Rings held more value than rose-petals to be strewn over the carpeted aisle.

'You can have the basket.' Emily, too, had done her own calculations.

Teresa rolled her eyes, the girls' respective mothers attempted to pacify, and when that failed they tried bribery.

The four bridesmaids looked tense, for they'd each been assigned a child to care for during the formal ceremony.

'OK.' Aysha lifted both hands in a gesture of expressive defeat. 'This is how it's going to be. Two baskets, so Emily and Samantha get to carry one each.' She cast both boys a stern look. 'Two pillows.'

'Two?' Teresa queried incredulously, and Aysha inclined her head.

'Two.'

The little girls beamed, and both boys bent their heads in sulky disagreement.

Maybe it would have been wiser not to give the children a rehearsal at all, and simply tell them what to do on the day and hope they'd concentrate so hard there wouldn't be the opportunity for error.

Celestial assistance was obviously going to be needed, Aysha mused as she listened to the priest's instructions.

An hour later they were all seated at a long table in a restaurant nominated as children-friendly. The food was good, the wine did much to relax fraught nerves, and Aysha enjoyed the informality of it all as she leaned back against Carlo's supporting arm.

'Tired?'

She lifted her face to his, and her eyes sparkled with latent intimacy. 'It's been a long day.'

He leaned in close and brushed his lips to her temple. 'You can sleep in in the morning.'

'Generous of you. But I need to be home early to help Teresa with preparations for the bridal shower. Remember?'

It was almost eleven when everyone began to make a move, and a further half-hour before Aysha and Carlo were able to leave, for the bridesmaids lingered and Teresa had last-minute instructions to impart.

The witching hour of midnight struck as she preceded Carlo into the penthouse, and she slipped off her shoes, took the clip from her hair and shook it loose, then she padded through to the kitchen.

'Coffee?'

Aysha sensed rather than heard him move behind her, and she murmured her approval as his hands kneaded tense shoulder muscles.

'Good?'

Oh, yes. So good, she was prepared to beg him to continue. 'Please. Don't stop.' It was bliss, almost heaven, and she closed her eyes as his fingers worked a magic all on their own.

'Any ideas for tomorrow night?'

She heard the lazy quality in his voice and smiled. 'You mean we have a free evening?'

'I can book dinner.'

'Don't,' she said at once. 'I'll pick up something.'

'I could do this much better if you lay down on the bed.'

Her senses were heightened, and her pulse began to quicken. 'That might prove dangerous.'

'Eventually,' Carlo agreed lazily. 'But there are advantages to a full body massage.'

Aysha's blood pressure moved up a notch. 'Are you seducing me?'

His soft laughter sounded deep and husky close to her ear. 'Am I succeeding?'

'I'll let you know,' she promised with wicked intent. 'In about an hour from now.'

'An hour?'

'The quality of the massage will govern your reward,' Aysha informed him solemnly, and he laughed as he swept her into his arms and carried her through to the bedroom.

To lay prone on towels as Carlo slowly smoothed aromatic oil over every inch of her body was sensual torture of the sweetest kind.

Whatever had made her think she'd last an hour? After thirty minutes the pleasure was so intense, it was all she could do not to roll onto her back and beg him to take her.

'I think,' she said between gritted teeth, 'that's enough.'

His fingertips smoothed up her thighs and lingered a hair's breadth away from the apex, then shaped each buttock before settling at her waist.

'You said an hour,' Carlo reminded her, and gently rolled her onto her back.

Aysha looked at him from beneath long-fringed

lashes. 'I'll make you pay,' she promised as liquid heat spilled through her veins.

He leaned down and took her mouth in a brief hard kiss. 'I'm counting on it.'

The sweet sorcery of his touch nearly sent her mad, and afterwards it was she who drove him to the brink, aware of those dark eyes watching her with an almost predatory alertness that gradually shifted and changed as she tried to break his control.

Desire, raw and primitive, tore through her body, and she felt bare, exposed, as her own fragile control shredded into a thousand pieces.

Aysha had no recollection of the tears that slowly spilled down each cheek until Carlo cupped her face and erased them with a single movement of his thumb.

His lips brushed hers, gently, back and forth, then angled in sensual possession.

Afterwards he simply held her until her breathing slowed and steadied into a regular beat, then he gently eased her to lie beside him and held her close through the night.

She barely stirred when he rose at eight, and he showered in a spare bathroom, then dressed and made breakfast.

The aroma of freshly brewed coffee stirred Aysha's senses, and she fought through the final mists of sleep into wakefulness.

'The tousled look suits you,' Carlo teased as he placed the tray down onto the bedside pedestal. Her cheeks were softly flushed, her eyes slumberous, the dilated pupils making them seem too large for her face.

'Hi.' She made an attempt to pull the sheet a little higher, and incurred his husky laughter.

'Your modesty is adorable, *cara*.'

'Breakfast in bed,' she murmured appreciatively. 'You've excelled yourself.'

He lowered his head and bestowed an open-mouthed kiss to the edge of her throat, teased the tender skin with his teeth, then trailed a path to the gentle swell of her breast.

'I aim to please.'

Oh, yes, he did that. She retained a very vivid memory of just how well he'd managed to please her. Not that it had been entirely one-sided… She'd managed to take him further towards the edge than before. One of these days…*nights*, she amended, she planned to tip him over and watch him free-fall.

'Naturally, your mind is more on food than me at this point, hmm?'

Go much lower, and I won't get to the food. 'Of course,' she offered demurely. 'I'm going to need stamina to make it through the day.'

'The bridal shower,' he mused. His eyes met hers, and she regarded him solemnly.

'Teresa wants the occasion to be memorable.'

Carlo sank down onto the bed. 'There's orange juice, and caffeine to kick-start the day.'

Together with toast, croissants, fruit preserve, cheese, wafer-thin slices of salami and prosciutto. A veritable feast.

Aysha slid up in the bed, paying careful attention

to keep the sheet tucked beneath her arms, and took the glass of juice from Carlo's extended hand. Next came the coffee, then a croissant with preserve, followed by a piece of toast folded in half over a layer of cheese and prosciutto.

'More coffee?'

She hesitated, checked the time, then shook her head. 'I said I'd be home around nine.'

Carlo stood to his feet and collected the tray. 'I'll take this downstairs.'

Ten minutes later she had showered, dressed and was ready to face the day. Light blue jeans sheathed her slim legs, hugged her hips, and she wore a fitted top that accentuated the delicate curve of her breasts.

She skirted the servery, reached up and planted a light kiss against the edge of his jaw. 'Thanks for breakfast.'

He caught her close and slanted his mouth over hers with a possession that wreaked havoc with her equilibrium. Then he eased the pressure and brushed his lips over the swollen contours of her own, lingered at one corner, then gently released her.

'I consider myself thanked.'

Her eyes felt too large, and she quickly blinked in an effort to clear her vision. That had been... 'cataclysmic' was a word that came immediately to mind. And passionate, definitely passionate.

Maybe she was beginning to scratch the surface of his control after all.

That thought stayed with her as she took the lift down to the underground car park, and during the few kilometres to her parents' home.

CHAPTER THREE

AYSHA'S four bridesmaids were the first to arrive, followed by Gianna and a few of Teresa's friends. Two aunts, three cousins, and a number of close friends.

There were beautifully wrapped gifts, much laughter, a little wine, some champagne, and the exchange of numerous anecdotes. Entertainment was provided by a gifted magician whose expertise in pulling at least a hundred scarves from his hat and jacket pockets had to be seen to be believed.

Coffee was served at three-thirty, and at four Teresa was summoned to the front door to accept the arrival of an unexpected guest.

The speed with which Lianna, Aysha' chief bridesmaid, joined Teresa aroused suspicion, and there was much laughter as a good-looking young man entered the lounge.

'You didn't—' Aysha began, and one look at Lianna, Arianne, Suzanne and Tessa was sufficient to determine that her four bridesmaids were as guilty as sin.

A portable tape-recorder was set on a coffee table, and when the music began he went into a series of choreographed movements as he began to strip.

It was a tastefully orchestrated act, as such acts went. The young man certainly had the frame, the body, the muscles to execute the traditional bump-and-grind routine.

'You refused to let us give you a ladies' night out, so we had to do something,' Lianna confided with an impish grin as everyone began to leave.

'Fiend,' Aysha chastised with affectionate remonstrance. 'Wait until it's your turn.'

'What'll you do to top it, Aysha? Hire a group of male strippers?'

'Don't put thoughts into my head,' she threatened direly.

The caterers tidied and cleaned up, then left fifteen minutes later, and Aysha crossed to the table where a selection of gifts were on display.

From the intensely practical to the highly decorative, they were all beautiful and reflected the giver's personality. A smile curved her lips. Lianna's gift of a male stripper had been the wackiest.

'You had no idea of Lianna's surprise?' Teresa queried as she crossed to her side.

'None,' Aysha answered truthfully, and curved an arm around her mother's waist. 'Thanks, Mamma, for a lovely afternoon.'

'My pleasure.'

Aysha grinned unashamedly. 'Even the stripper?' she teased, and glimpsed the faint pink colour in her mother's cheeks.

'No comment.'

She began to laugh. 'All right, let's change the subject. What shall we do with these gifts?'

They set them on a table in one of the rooms Teresa had organised for displaying the wedding presents, and when that was done Aysha went upstairs and changed into tailored trousers and matching silk top.

It was after six when she entered Carlo's penthouse apartment, and she crossed directly into the kitchen to deposit the carry-sack containing a selection of Chinese takeaways she'd collected *en route* from home.

'Let me guess. Chinese, Thai, Malaysian?' Carlo drawled as he entered the kitchen, and she directed him a winsome smile.

'Chinese. And I picked up some videos.'

'You have plans to spend a quiet night?'

She opened cupboards and extracted two plates, then collected cutlery. 'I think I've had enough excitement for the day.' And through last night.

'Care to elaborate on the afternoon?'

Her eyes sparkled with hidden devilry. 'Lianna ordered a male stripper.' She decided to tease him a little. 'He was young, *built*, and gorgeous.' She wrinkled her nose at him. 'Ask Gianna; she was there.'

'Indeed?' His eyes speared hers. 'Perhaps I need to hear more about this gorgeous hunk.'

Carlo had her heart, her soul. It never ceased to hurt that she didn't have his.

'Well...' She deliberated. 'There was the body to die for.' She ticked off each attribute with teasing relish. 'Longish hair, tied in this cute little ponytail, and when he let it free...wow, so sexy. No apparent body hair.' Her eyes sparkled with devilish humour. 'Waxing must be a pain...literally. And he had the cutest butt.'

Carlo's eyes narrowed fractionally, and she gave him an irrepressible grin. 'He stripped down to a thong bikini brief.'

'I imagine Teresa and Gianna were relieved.'

She tried hard not to laugh, and failed as a chuckle emerged. 'They appeared to enjoy the show.'

His lips twitched. 'An unexpected show, unless I'm mistaken.'

'Totally,' she agreed, and viewed the various cartons she'd deposited on the servery. 'Let's be *really* decadent,' she suggested lightly. 'And watch a video while we eat.'

The first was a thriller, the acting sufficiently superb to bring an audience to the edge of their seats, and the second was a comedy about a wedding where everything that could go wrong, did. It was funny, slapstick, and over the top, but in amongst the frivolity was a degree of reality Aysha could identify with.

In between videos she'd tidied cartons and rinsed plates, made coffee, and now she carried the cups through to the kitchen.

She felt pleasantly tired as she ascended the stairs to the main bedroom, and after a quick shower she slid between the sheets to curl comfortably in the circle of Carlo's arms with her head pillowed against his chest.

Within minutes she fell asleep, and she was unaware of the light touch as Carlo's lips brushed the top of her head, or the feather-light trail of his fingers as they smoothed a path over the surface of her skin.

They woke late, lingered over breakfast, then took

Giuseppe's cabin cruiser for a day trip up the Hawkesbury River. They returned as the sun set in a glorious flare of fading colour and the cityscape sprang to life with a myriad of pin-prick lights.

Magic, Aysha reflected, as the wonder of nature and manmade technology overwhelmed her.

Tomorrow the shopping would begin in earnest as Teresa initiated the first of her many lists of Things to Do.

'Mamma, is this really necessary?'

As shopping went, it had been a profitable day with regard to acquisitions. Teresa, it appeared, was bent on spending money... *Serious* money.

'You're the only child I have,' Teresa said simply. 'Don't deny me the pleasure of giving my daughter the best wedding I can provide.'

Aysha tucked her hand through her mother's arm and hugged it close. 'Don't rain on my parade, huh?'

'Exactly.'

'OK. The dress, if you insist. But...' She paused, and cast Teresa a stern look. 'That's it,' she admonished.

'For today.'

They joined the exodus of traffic battling to exit choked city streets, and made it to Vaucluse at five-thirty, leaving very little time to shower, change and be ready to leave the house at six thirty.

'You go on ahead,' Teresa suggested. 'I'll put these in the room next to yours. We can sort through them tomorrow.'

Aysha raced upstairs to her bedroom, then discarded her clothes and made for the shower. Minutes later she wound a towel round her slim curves, removed the excess moisture from her hair and wielded the hairdrier to good effect.

Basic make-up followed, then she crossed to the walk-in robe, cast a quick discerning eye over the carefully co-ordinated contents, and extracted a figure-hugging gown in black.

The hemline rested at mid-thigh, the overall length extended slightly by a wide border of scalloped lace. The design was sleeveless, backless, and cunningly styled to show a modest amount of cleavage. Thin shoulder straps ensured the gown stayed in place.

Sheer black pantyhose? Or should she settle for bare legs and almost non-existent thong bikini briefs? And very high stiletto-heeled pumps?

Minimum jewellery, she decided, and she'd sweep her hair into a casual knot atop her head.

Half an hour later she descended the stairs to the lower floor and entered the lounge. Teresa and Giuseppe were grouped together sharing a light aperitif.

Her father turned towards her, his expression a comedic mix of parental pride and male appreciation. Any hint of paternal remonstrance was absent, doubtless on the grounds that his beloved daughter was safely spoken for, on the verge of marriage, and therefore he had absolutely nothing to worry about.

Teresa, however, was something else. One glance was all it took for those dark eyes to narrow fractionally and the lips to thin. *Appearance* was everything, and tonight Aysha did not fit her mother's required image.

'Don't you think that's a little…?' Teresa paused delicately. 'Bold, darling?'

'Perhaps,' Aysha conceded, and directed her father a teasing glance. 'Papà?'

Giuseppe was well versed in the ways of mother and daughter, and sought a diplomatic response. 'I'm sure Carlo will be most appreciative.' He gestured towards a crystal decanter. 'Can I fix you a spritzer?'

She hadn't eaten much throughout the day, just nibbled on fresh fruit, sipped several glasses of water, and taken three cups of long black coffee. Alcohol would go straight to her head. 'I stopped by the kitchen when I arrived home and fixed some juice,' she declined gently. 'I'm fine.'

'Unless I'm mistaken, that's Carlo now.'

The light crunch of car tires, the faint clunk of a door closing, followed by the distant sound of melodic door chimes heralded his arrival, and within seconds their live-in housekeeper ushered him into the lounge.

Aysha crossed the room and caught hold of his hand, then offered her cheek for his kiss. It was a natural gesture, one that was expected, and only she heard the light teasing murmur close to her ear. 'Stunning.'

His arm curved round the back of her waist and he drew her with him as he moved to accept Teresa's greeting.

'A drink, Carlo?'

'I'll wait until dinner.'

It would be easy to lean in against him, and for a moment she almost did. Except there was no one to impress, and the evening lay ahead.

Giuseppe swallowed the remainder of his wine, and placed his glass down onto the tray. 'In that case, perhaps we should be on our way. Teresa?'

At that moment the phone rang, and Teresa frowned in disapproval. 'I hope that's not going to make us late.'

Not unless the call heralded something of dire consequence; there wasn't a chance. Aysha bit back on the mockery, and sensed her mother's words even before they were uttered.

'You and Carlo go on ahead. We won't be far behind you.'

Sliding into the passenger seat of the car was achieved with greater decorum than she expected, and she was in the process of fastening her seatbelt when Carlo moved behind the wheel.

A deft flick of his wrist and the engine purred to life. Almost a minute later they had traversed the curved driveway and were heading towards the city.

'Am I correct in assuming the dress is a desire to shock?'

Aysha heard the drawling voice, sensed the underlying cynicism tinged with humour, and turned to look at him. 'Does it succeed?'

She was supremely conscious of the amount of bare thigh showing, and she fought against the temptation to take hold of the hemline and attempt to tug it down.

He turned slightly towards her, and in that second

she was acutely aware of the darkness of his eyes, the faint curve of his mouth, the gleam of white teeth.

'Teresa didn't approve.'

'You know her so well,' she indicated wryly. 'Papà seemed to think you'd be appreciative.'

'Oh, I am,' Carlo declared. 'As I'm sure every other man in the room will be.'

She directed him a stunning smile. 'You say the nicest things.'

'Careful you don't overdo it, *cara*.'

'I'm aiming for brilliance.'

For one brief second her eyes held the faintest shadow, then it was gone. He lifted a hand and brushed light fingers down her cheek.

'A few hours, four at the most. Then we can leave.'

Yes, she thought sadly. And tomorrow it will start all over again. The shopping, fittings, social obligations. Each day it seemed to get worse. Fulfilling her mother's expectations, having her own opinions waved aside, the increasing tension. If only Teresa wasn't bent on turning everything into such a *production*.

Suburban Point Piper was a neighbouring suburb and took only minutes to reach.

Carlo turned between ornate wrought-iron gates and parked behind a stylish Jaguar. Four, no, five cars lined the curved driveway, and Aysha experienced a moment's hesitation as she moved towards the few steps leading to the main entrance.

There had been countless precedents of an evening

such as this, Aysha reflected as she accepted a light wine and exchanged pleasantries with fellow guests.

Beautiful home, gracious host and hostess. The requisite mingling over drinks for thirty minutes before dinner. Any number between ten to twenty guests, a splendid table. An exquisite floral centrepiece. The guests carefully selected to complement each other.

'Carlo, *darling*.'

Aysha heard the greeting, recognised the sultry feminine purr, and turned slowly to face one of several women who had worked hard to win Carlo's affection.

Now that the wedding was imminent, most had retired gracefully from the hunt. With the exception of Nina di Salvo.

The tall, svelte fashion consultant was a *femme fatale*, wealthy, widowed, and selectively seeking a husband of equal wealth and social standing.

Nina was admired, even adored, by men. For her style, beauty and wit. Women recognised the predatory element existent, and reacted accordingly.

'Aysha,' Nina acknowledged. 'You look...' The pause was deliberate. 'A little tired. All the preparations getting to you, darling?'

Aysha summoned a winsome smile and honed the proverbial dart. 'Carlo doesn't permit me enough sleep.'

Nina's eyes narrowed fractionally, then she leaned towards Carlo, brushed her lips against his cheek, and lingered a fraction too long. 'How are you, *caro*?'

'Nina.' Carlo was too skilful a strategist to give anything away, and too much the gentleman to do other than observe the social niceties.

He handled Nina's overt affection with practised ease and minimum body contact. Although Nina more than made up for his reticence, Aysha noted, wondering just how he regarded the glamorous brunette's attention.

She saw his smile, heard his laughter, and felt the tender care of his touch. Yet how much was a façade?

'Do get me a drink, *caro*,' Nina commanded lightly. 'You know what I like.'

Oh, my, Aysha determined as Carlo excused himself and made his way to the bar. This could turn into one hell of an evening.

'I hope you don't expect fidelity, darling,' Nina warned quietly. 'Carlo has...' she paused fractionally '...certain needs not every woman would be happy to fulfil.'

Cut straight to the chase, a tiny voice prompted. 'Really, Nina? I'll broach that with him.'

'What will you broach, and with whom?'

Speak of the devil... Aysha turned towards him as he handed Nina a slim flute of champagne.

Quite deliberately she tilted her chin and gazed into his dark gleaming eyes with amused serenity. She'd had plenty of *smile* practice, and she proffered one of pseudo-sincerity. 'Nina expressed her concern regarding my ability to fulfil your needs.'

Carlo's expression didn't change, and Aysha

dimly registered that as a poker player he would be almost without equal.

'Really?'

It seemed difficult to comprehend a single word could hold such a wealth of meaning. Or the quiet tone convey such a degree of cold anger.

The tension was evident, although Carlo hadn't moved so much as a muscle. Anyone viewing the scene would assume the three of them were engaged in pleasant conversation.

'Perhaps Nina and I should get together and compare notes,' Aysha declared with wicked humour.

Nina lifted the flute to her lips and took a delicate sip. 'What for, darling? My notes are bound to be far more extensive than yours.'

Wasn't that the truth? She caught a glimpse of aqua silk and saw Teresa and Giuseppe enter the room, and wasn't sure whether to be relieved or disappointed at their appearance.

Her mother would assess Nina's presence in an instant, and seek to break up their happy little threesome.

Aysha began a silent countdown... Three minutes to greet their hosts, another three to acknowledge a few friends.

'There you are, darling.'

Right on cue. Aysha turned towards her mother and proffered an affectionate smile. 'Mamma. You weren't held up too long, after all.' She indicated the tall brunette. 'You remember Nina?'

Teresa eyes sharpened, although her features bore

a charming smile. 'Of course. How nice to see you again.'

A lie, if ever there was one. Polite society, Aysha mused. Good manners hid a multitude of sins. If she were to obey her base instincts, she'd tell Nina precisely where to go and how to complete the journey.

There was an inherent need to show her claws, but this wasn't the time or place.

'Shall we go in to dinner?'

A respite, Aysha determined with a sense of relief. Unless their hostess had chosen unwisely and placed Nina in close proximity.

The dining room was large, the focal point being the perfectly set table positioned beneath a sparkling crystal chandelier of exquisite design.

The scene resembled a photograph lifted out of the social pages of a glossy magazine. It seemed almost a sacrilege for guests to spoil the splendid placement precision.

Although there were, she noted, a waiter and waitress present to serve allotted food portions at pre-arranged intervals. Likewise the imported wine would flow, but not at a rate that was considered too free.

Respectability, decorum, an adherence to exemplary good manners, with carefully orchestrated conversational topics guaranteed to stimulate the guests' interest.

Aysha caught Nina's gleam of silent mockery, and had an insane desire to disrupt it. A little, just a little.

Nothing overt, she decided as she selected a spoon

and dipped it into the part-filled bowl of mushroom soup.

The antipasto offered a superb selection, and the serving of linguini with its delicate cream and mushroom sauce couldn't be faulted.

'Could you have the waiter pour me some wine, darling?' Aysha cast Carlo a stunning smile. She rarely drank alcohol, and he knew it. However, she figured she had sufficient food in her stomach to filter the effect if she sipped it slowly.

Her request resulted in a slanted eyebrow, and she offered him the sweetest smile. 'Please.'

If he hesitated, or attempted to censure her in any way, she'd kill him.

A glance was all it took for the waiter to fill her glass, and seconds later she lifted the crystal flute to her lips and savoured the superb Chablis.

Giuseppe smiled, and lifted his own glass in a silent salute.

A few glasses of fine wine, good food, pleasant company. It took little to please her father. He was a man of simple tastes. He had worked hard all his life, achieved more than most men; he owned a beautiful home, had chosen a good woman as his wife, and together they had raised a wonderful daughter who was soon to be married to the son of his best friend and business partner. His life was good. Very good.

Dear Papà, Aysha thought fondly as the wine began to have a mellowing effect. He was everything a father should be, and more. A man who had managed to blend the best of the Old Country with the best of the new. The result was a miscible blend of wisdom and warmth tempered with pride and passion.

The main course was served...tender breast of chicken in a delicate basil sauce with an assortment of vegetables.

Her elbow touched Carlo's arm, and she lowered her hand to her lap as she unconsciously toyed with her napkin. His thigh was close to her own. Very close.

Slowly, very slowly, she moved her leg until it rested against his. It would be so easy to glide her foot over his. With extreme care, she cautioned silently. Stiletto heels as fine as hers should almost be registered as a dangerous weapon. The idea was to arouse his attention, not cause him an injury.

Gently she positioned the toe of her shoe against his ankle, then inched it slowly back and forth without moving her heel, thereby making it impossible for anyone to detect what she was doing.

This could be fun, she determined as she let her fingers slide towards his thigh. A butterfly touch, fleeting.

Should she be more daring? Perhaps run the tip of her manicured fingernail down the outer seam of the trousered leg so close to her own? Maybe even...

Ah, that brought a reaction. Slight, but evident, nonetheless. And the slight but warning squeeze of his fingers as they caught hold of her own.

Aysha met his gaze fearlessly as he turned towards her, and she glimpsed the musing indolence apparent beneath the gleaming warmth of those dark brown depths.

Without missing a beat, he lifted her hand to his lips and kissed each finger in turn, watching the way her eyes dilated in startled surprise. Then he returned her hand to rest on his thigh, tracing a slow pattern over the fine bones, aware of her slight tremor as he deliberately forestalled her effort to pull free.

It was fortunate they were between courses. Aysha looked at the remaining wine in her glass, and opted for chilled water. Wisdom decreed the need for a clear head. Each brush of his fingers sent flame licking through her veins, and she clenched her hand, then dug her nails into hard thigh muscle in silent entreaty.

She experienced momentary relief when Carlo released her hand, only to suppress a faint gasp as she felt his fingers close over her thigh.

CHAPTER FOUR

AYSHA reached for her glass and took a sip of iced water, and cast the table's occupants a quick, encompassing glance.

Her eyes rested briefly on Nina, witnessed her hard, calculating glance before it was quickly masked, and felt a shiver glide down the length of her spine.

Malevolence, no matter how fleeting, was disconcerting. Envy and jealousy in others were unenviable traits, and something she'd learned to deal with from a young age. It had accelerated with her engagement to Carlo. Doubtless it would continue long after the marriage.

She wanted love...desperately. But she'd settle for fidelity. Even the thought that he might look seriously at another woman made it feel as if a hand took hold of her heart and squeezed until it bled.

'What do you think, Aysha?'

Oh, hell. It wasn't wise to allow distraction to interfere with the thread of social conversation. Especially not when you were a guest of honour.

She looked at Carlo with a silent plea for help, and met his humorous gaze.

'Luisa doesn't agree I should keep our honeymoon destination a surprise.'

A second was all it took to summon a warm smile.

'I need to pack warm clothes.' Her eyes gleamed and a soft laugh escaped her lips. 'That's all I know.'

'Europe. The snowfields?' The older woman's eyes twinkled. 'Maybe North America. Canada?'

'I really have no idea,' Aysha declared.

Dessert comprised individual caramelised baskets filled with segments of fresh fruit served with brandied cream.

'Sinful,' Aysha declared quietly as she savoured a delectable mouthful.

'I shouldn't, but I will,' Luisa uttered ruefully. 'Tomorrow I'll compensate with fresh juice for breakfast and double my gym workout.'

Teresa, she noted, carefully removed the cream, speared a few segments of fruit, and left the candied basket. As mother of the bride, she couldn't afford to add even a fraction of a kilo to her svelte figure.

It was half an hour before the hostess requested they move into the lounge for coffee.

Aysha declined the very strong espresso brew and opted for a much milder blend with milk. The men took it short and sweet, added *grappa*, and converged together to exchange opinions on anything from *bocce* to the state of the government.

Argue, Aysha amended fondly, all too aware that familiar company, good food, fine wine all combined to loosen the male Italian tongue and encourage reminiscence.

She loved to listen to the cadence of their voices as they lapsed into the language of their birth. It was expressive, accompanied by the philosophical shrug of masculine shoulders, the hand movements to emphasise a given point.

'Giuseppe is in his element.'

Aysha mentally prepared herself as she turned to face Nina. One glance was all it took to determine Nina's manner was the antithesis of friendly.

'Is there any reason why he shouldn't be?'

'The wedding is a major coup.' The smile didn't reach her eyes. 'Congratulations, darling. I should have known you'd pull it off.'

Aysha inclined her head. 'Thank you, Nina. I'll take that as a compliment.'

There was no one close enough to overhear the quiet exchange. Which was a pity. It merely offered Nina the opportunity to aim another poisoned dart.

'How does it feel to be second-best? And know your inherited share in the family firm is the sole reason for the marriage?'

'Considering Carlo is due to inherit his share in the family firm, perhaps you should ask him the same question.'

Successfully fielded. Nina didn't like it. Her eyes narrowed, and the smile moved up a notch in artificial brilliance.

'You're the one who has to compete with Bianca's ghost,' Nina offered silkily, and Aysha waited for the punchline. 'All cats are alike in the dark, darling. Didn't you know?'

Oh, my. This was getting dirty. 'Really?' Her cheeks hurt from keeping a smile pinned in place. 'Perhaps you should try it with the lights on, some time.'

As scores went, it hardly rated a mention. And the victory was short-lived, for it was doubtful Nina would allow anyone to gain an upper hand for long.

'Aysha.' Luisa appeared at her side. 'Teresa has just been telling me about the flowers for the church. Orchids make a lovely display, and the colour combination will be exquisite.'

She was a guest of honour, the focus her wedding day. It was easy to slip into animated mode and discuss details. Only the wedding dress and the cake were taboo.

Except talking and answering questions merely reinforced how much there still was to do, and how essential the liaison with the wedding organiser Teresa had chosen to co-ordinate everything.

The invitation responses were all in, the seating arrangements were in their final planning stage. According to Teresa, any one of the two little flower girls and two page boys could fall victim to a malicious virus, or contract mumps, measles or chicken pox. Alternately, one or all could become paralysed with fright on the day and freeze half-way down the aisle.

At ages three and four, anything was possible.

'My flower girl scattered rose petals down the aisle perfectly at rehearsal, only to take three steps forward on the day, tip the entire contents of the basket on the carpet, and run crying to her mother,' recalled one of the guests.

Aysha remembered the incident, and another wedding where the page boy had carried the satin ring-cushion with such pride and care, then refused to give it up at the appropriate moment. A tussle had ensued, followed by tears and a tantrum.

It had been amusing at the time, and she really didn't care if one of the children made a mistake, or missed their cue. It was a wedding, not a movie which relied on talented actors to perform a part.

Her mother, she knew, didn't hold the same view.

Aysha glanced towards Carlo, and felt the familiar pull of her senses. Dark, well-groomed hair, a strong shaped head. Broad shoulders accentuated by perfect tailoring.

A slight inclination of his head brought his profile into focus. The wide, sculpted bone structure, the strong jaw. Well-defined cheekbones, and the glimpse of his mouth.

Fascinated, she watched each movement, her eyes clinging to the shape of him, aware just how he felt without the constriction of clothes. She was familiar with his body's musculature, the feel and scent of his skin.

At this precise moment she would have given anything to cross to his side and have his arm curve round her waist. She could lean in against him, and savour the anticipation of what would happen when they were alone.

He was fond of her, she knew. There were occasions when he completely disconcerted her by appearing to read her mind. But that special empathy between two lovers wasn't there. No matter how desperately she wanted it to be.

Did he know she could tell the moment he entered a room? She didn't have to see him, or hear his voice. A developed sixth sense alerted her of his presence, and her body reacted as if he'd reached out and touched her.

All the fine hairs moved on the surface of her skin, and the back of her neck tingled in recognition.

Damnable, she cursed silently.

It was after eleven when the first of the guests took their leave, and almost midnight when Teresa and Giuseppe indicated an intention to depart.

Aysha thanked their hosts, smiled until her face hurt, and quivered slightly when Carlo caught hold of her hand as they followed her parents down the steps to their respective cars.

'Goodnight, darling.' Teresa leaned forward and brushed her daughter's cheek.

Aysha stood as Carlo unlocked the car, then she slid into the passenger seat, secured her belt, and leaned back against the headrest as Carlo fired the engine.

'Tired?'

She was conscious of his discerning glance seconds before he set the car in motion.

'A little.' She closed her eyes, and let the vehicle's movement and the quietness of the night seep into her bones.

'Do you want me to take you home?'

A silent sigh escaped her lips, and she effected a rueful smile. 'Now there's a question. Which home are you talking about? Yours, mine or ours?'

'The choice is yours.'

Was it? The new house was completely furnished, and awaiting only the final finishing touches. Her own bedroom beckoned, but that was fraught with implication Teresa would query in the morning.

Besides, she coveted the touch of his hands, the feel of his body, his mouth devastating her own.

Then she could pretend that good lovemaking was a substitute for *love*. That no one was meant to have it all, and in Carlo, their future together, she had more than her share.

'The penthouse.'

Carlo didn't comment, and she wondered if it would have made any difference if she'd said *home*.

An ache started up in the pit of her stomach, and intensified until it became a tangible pain as he slowed the car, de-activated the security system guarding entrance to the luxury apartment building, then eased down into the underground car park and brought the vehicle to a halt in his allotted space.

They rode the lift to the top floor in silence, and inside the apartment Aysha went willingly into his arms, his bed, an eager supplicant to anything he chose to bestow.

It was just after nine when Aysha eased the Porsche into an empty space in an inner city car park building, and within minutes she stepped off the escalator and emerged onto the pavement.

It was a beautiful day, the sky a clear azure with hardly a cloud in sight, and the sun's warmth bathed all beneath it with a balmy summer brilliance. Her needs were few, the purchases confined to four boutiques, three of which were within three blocks of each other.

Two hours, tops, she calculated, then she'd meet her bridesmaids for lunch. At two she had a hair appointment, followed by a manicure, and tonight she was attending an invitation-only preview of the first in a series of foreign films scheduled to appear over the next month.

Each evening there was something filling their social engagement diary. Although last night when Carlo had suggested dining out she'd insisted they eat in...and somehow the decision hadn't got made one way or the other. She retained a vivid recollection of *why*, and a secret smile curved her lips as she slid her sunglasses into place.

Selecting clothes was something she enjoyed, and she possessed a natural flair for colour, fashion and design.

Aysha had three hours before she was due to join her bridesmaids for lunch, and she intended to utilise that time to its fullest potential.

It was nice to be able to take time, instead of having to rush in a limited lunch-hour. Selective shopping was fun, and she gradually added to a growing collection of glossy carry-bags.

Bags she should really dispense with before meeting the girls...which meant a walk back to the car park to deposit her purchases in the boot of her car.

Lianna, Arianne, Suzanne and Tessa were already seated when Aysha joined them. Two brunettes, a redhead, and a blonde. They'd attended school together, suffered through piano and ballet lessons, and, although their characters were quite different from each other, they shared an empathy that had firmed over the years as an unbreakable bond.

'You're late, but we forgive you,' Lianna began before Aysha was able to say a word. 'Of course, we do understand.' She offered one of her irrepressible smiles. 'You have serious shopping on the agenda.' She leaned forward. 'And your penance is to relay every little detail.'

'Let me order a drink first,' Aysha protested, and gave her order to a hovering waiter. 'Mineral water, slice of lemon, plenty of ice.'

'What did you buy to change into after the wedding?' Arianne quizzed, and Lianna pulled a face.

'Sweetheart, she won't *need* anything to wear after the wedding except skin.'

'Sure. But she should have something sheer and sexy to start off with,' Suzanne interceded.

'Honest, girls, can you see Carlo helping Aysha out of the wedding gown and into a nightgown? Come on, let's get real here!'

'Are you done?' Aysha queried, trying to repress a threatening laugh.

'Not yet,' Lianna declared blithely. 'You need to suffer a little pain for all the trouble we're going to for you.' She began counting them off on each finger. 'Dress fittings, shoe shopping, church rehearsals, child chaperoning, in church and out of it, organising the bridal shower, not to mention make-up sessions and hair stylists practising on our hair.' Her eyes sparkled with devilish laughter. 'For all of which our only reward is to kiss the groom.'

'Who said you get to do that?' Aysha queried with

mock seriousness. 'Married men don't kiss other women.'

'No kiss, we decorate the wedding car,' Lianna threatened.

'Are you ladies ready to order?'

'Yes,' they agreed in unison, and proceeded to completely confuse the poor young man who'd been assigned to their table.

'You're incorrigible,' Aysha chastised as soon as he'd disappeared towards the kitchen, and Lianna gave a conciliatory shrug.

'This is a *feel-good* moment, darling. The last of the great single-women luncheons. Saturday week you join the ranks of married ladies, while we, poor darlings, languish on the sideline searching for the perfect man. Of which, believe me, there are very few.' She paused to draw breath. 'If they look good, they sound terrible, or have disgusting habits, or verge towards violence, or, worst of all, have no money.'

Suzanne shook her head. 'Cynical, way too cynical.'

They ordered another round of drinks, then their food arrived.

'So, tell us, darling,' Lianna cajoled. 'Is Carlo as gorgeous in bed as he is out of it?'

'That's a bit below the belt,' Arianne protested, and Lianna grinned.

'Got it in one. Hey, if Aysha ditches him, I'm next in line.' She cast Aysha a wicked wink. 'Aren't you glad I'm your best friend?'

'Yes,' she responded simply. Loyalty and integrity

mattered, and Lianna possessed both, even if she was an irrepressible motor-mouth. The fun, the generous smile hid a childhood marred by tragedy.

'You haven't told us what you bought this morning.'

'You didn't give me a chance.'

'I'm giving it to you now,' Lianna insisted magnanimously, and Aysha laughed.

She needed the levity, and it was good, so good to relax and unwind among friends.

'What social event is scheduled for tonight? Dinner with family, the theatre, ballet, party? Or do you just get to stay home and go to bed with Carlo?'

'You have the cheek of old Nick,' Aysha declared, and caught Lianna's wicked smile.

'You didn't answer the question.'

'There's a foreign film festival on at the Arts Centre.'

'Ah, eclectic entertainment,' Arianne sighed wistfully. 'What are you going to wear?'

'Something utterly gorgeous,' Lianna declared, her eyes narrowing speculatively. 'Long black evening trousers or skirt, matching top, shoestring straps, and that exquisite beaded evening jacket you picked up in Hong Kong. Minimum jewellery.'

'OK.'

'*OK?* I'm in fashion, darling. What I've just described is considerably higher on the scale of gorgeous than just *OK*.'

'All right, I'll wear it,' Aysha conceded peaceably.

They skipped dessert, ordered coffee, and Aysha barely made her hair appointment on time.

'No dinner for me, Mamma. I'll just pick up some fruit. I had a late lunch,' she relayed via the mobile phone prior to driving home. With the way traffic was moving, it would be six before she reached Vaucluse. Which would leave her just under an hour to shower, dress, tend to her hair and make-up, and be at Carlo's apartment by seven-fifteen.

'*Bella*,' he complimented warmly as she used her key barely minutes after the appointed time.

Aysha could have said the same, for he looked devastatingly attractive attired in a dark evening suit, snowy white cotton shirt, and black bow tie. Arresting, she added, aware of her body's reaction to his appreciative appraisal. Heat flooded her veins, activating all her nerve-ends, as she felt the magnetic pull of the senses. It would be so easy just to hold out her arms and walk into his, then lift her face for his kiss. She wanted to, badly.

'Would you like a drink before we leave?'

Alcohol on a near-empty stomach wasn't a good idea, and she shook her head. 'No. Thanks.'

'How was lunch with the girls?'

A smile lifted the edges of her mouth, and her eyes gleamed with remembered pleasure. 'Great. Really great.'

Carlo caught hold of her hand and lifted it to his lips. 'I imagine Lianna was at her irrepressible best?'

'It was nice just to sit, relax and laugh a little.' Her smile widened, and her eyes searched his. 'Lianna is looking forward to kissing the groom.'

Carlo pulled back the cuff of his jacket and checked his watch. 'Perhaps we should be on our way. Traffic will be heavy, and parking probably a problem.'

It was a gala evening, and a few of the city's social scions numbered among the guests. The female contingent wore a small fortune in jewels and French designer gowns vied with those by their Italian equivalent.

Aysha mingled with fellow guests, nibbled from a proffered tray of hors d'oeuvres, and sipped orange juice with an added dash of champagne.

'Sorry I'm a little late. Parking was chaotic.'

Aysha recognised the light feminine voice and turned to greet its owner. 'Hello, Nina.'

The brunette let her gaze trail down to the tips of Aysha's shoes, then slowly back again in a deliberately provocative assessment. 'Aysha, how—pretty, you look. Although black is a little stark, darling, on one as fair as you.'

She turned towards Carlo, and her smile alone could have lit up the entire auditorium. '*Caro*, I really need a drink. Do you think you could organise one for me?'

Very good, Aysha silently applauded. Wait for the second Carlo is out of earshot, and…any minute now—

'I doubt you'll satisfy him for long.'

Aysha met that piercing gaze and held it. She even managed a faint smile. 'I'll give it my best shot.'

'There are distinct advantages in having the wedding ring, I guess.'

'I get to sleep with him?'

Nina's eyes glittered. 'I'd rather be his mistress

than his wife, darling. That way I get most of the pleasure, all of the perks, while you do the time.'

The temptation to throw the contents of her glass in Nina's face was almost irresistible.

'Champagne?' Carlo drawled, handing Nina a slim flute.

The electronic tone summoning the audience to take their seats came as a welcome intrusion, and she made her way into the theatre at Carlo's side, all too aware of Nina's presence as the usherette pointed them in the direction of their seats.

Now why wasn't she surprised when Nina's seat allocation adjoined theirs? Hardly coincidence, and Aysha gritted her teeth when Nina very cleverly ensured Carlo took the centre seat. Grr.

The lights dimmed, and her fingers stiffened as Carlo covered her hand with his own. Worse was the soothing movement of his thumb against the inside of her wrist.

So he sensed her tension. Good. He'd sense a lot more before the evening was over!

The theatre lights went out, technicolor images filled the screen, and the previews of forthcoming movies showed in relatively quick sequence. The main feature was set in Paris, the French dubbed into English, and it was a dark movie, *noir*, with subjective nuances, no comedy whatsoever. Aysha found it depressing, despite the script, directorship and acting having won several awards.

The final scene climaxed with particular violence, and when the credits faded and the lights came on she saw Nina withdraw a hand from Carlo's forearm.

Aysha threw her an icy glare, glimpsed the glittering satisfaction evident, and wanted to scream.

She turned towards the aisle and moved with the flow of exiting patrons, aware, as if she was a disembodied spectator, that Nina took full advantage of the crowd situation to press as close to Carlo as decently possible.

They reached the auditorium foyer, and Aysha had to stand with a polite smile pinned to her face as the patrons were served coffee, offered cheese and biscuits or minuscule pieces of cake.

'Why don't we go on to a nightclub?' Nina suggested. 'It's not late.'

And watch you attempt to dance and play kissy-face with Carlo? Aysha demanded silently. Not if I have anything to do with it!

'Don't let us stop you,' Carlo declined smoothly as he curved an arm along the back of Aysha's waist. Tense, definitely tense. He wanted to bend his head and place a placating kiss to the curve of her neck, then look deep into those smoky grey eyes and silently assure her she had nothing whatsoever to worry about.

A slight smile curved his lips. Nina saw it, and misinterpreted its source.

'The music is incredible.' She tucked her hand through his arm, and cajoled with the guile of a temptress. 'You'll enjoy it.'

'No,' he declined in a silky voice as he carefully disengaged her hand. 'I won't.'

Nina recognised defeat when she saw it, and she

lifted her shoulders with an elegant shrug. 'If you must miss out...'

His raised eyebrow signalled her departure, and she swept him a deep sultry glance. 'Another time, maybe.'

Aysha drew a deep breath, then released it slowly. Of all the nerve! She lifted her cup and took a sip of ruinously strong coffee. It would probably keep her awake half the night, but right at this precise moment she didn't give a damn.

'Carlo, *come stai*?'

A business acquaintance, whose presence she welcomed with considerable enthusiasm. The man looked mildly stunned as she enquired about his wife, his children, their schooling and their achievements.

'You overwhelmed him,' Carlo declared with deceptive indolence, and she fixed him with a brilliant smile.

'His arrival was timely,' she assured him sweetly. 'I was about to hit you.'

'In public?'

She drew in a deep breath, and studied his features for several long seconds. 'This is not a time for levity.'

'Nina bothers you?'

Aysha forced herself to hold his gaze. 'She never misses an opportunity to be wherever we happen to go.'

His eyes narrowed fractionally. 'You think I don't know that?'

'Were you ever lovers?' she demanded, and a faint

chill feathered across the surface of her skin as she waited for his response.

'No.'

The words tripped out before she could stop them. 'You're quite sure about that?'

Carlo was silent for several seconds, then he ventured silkily, 'I've never been indiscriminate with the few women who've shared my bed. Believe me, Nina didn't number among them.' He took her cup and placed it together with his own on a nearby table.   'Shall we leave?'

He was angry, but then so was she, and she swept him a glittering look from beneath mascaraed lashes. 'Let's do that.'

Their passage to the car wasn't swift as they paused momentarily to chat to fellow patrons whom they knew or were acquainted with.

'Your silence is ominous,' Carlo remarked with droll humour as he eased the Mercedes into the flow of traffic.

'I'm going with the saying…*if you can't find anything nice to say, it's better to say nothing at all.*'

'I see.'

No, you don't. You couldn't possibly know how terrified I am of not being able to hold your interest. Petrified that one day you'll find someone else, and I'll be left a broken shell of my former self.

The drive from the city to Rose Bay was achieved in a relatively short space of time, and Carlo cleared security at his apartment underground car park, then manoeuvred the car into his allotted space.

Aysha released the door-clasp, slid to her feet,

closed the door, and moved the few steps to her car.

'What are you doing?'

'I would have thought that was obvious. I'm going home.'

'Your keys are in the apartment,' Carlo said mildly.

Dammit, so they were. 'In that case, I'll go get them.'

She turned and stalked towards the bank of lifts, stabbed the call button, and barely contained her impatience as she waited for it to arrive.

'Don't you think you're overreacting?'

There was something in his voice she failed to recognise, although some deep, inner sixth sense did and sent out a red alert. 'Not really.'

The doors slid open and she stepped into the cubicle, jabbed the top panel button, and stood in icy silence as they were transported to the uppermost floor.

Carlo unlocked the apartment door, and she swept in ahead of him, located the keys where she'd put them on a table in the foyer, and collected them.

'Your parents aren't expecting you back tonight.'

It didn't help that he was right. 'So I'll ring them.'

He noted the proud tilt of her chin, the firm set of her mouth. 'Stay.'

Her eyes flared. 'I'd prefer to go home.' Nina's vitriolic words had provided too vivid an image to easily dispel.

'I'll drive you.'

The inflexibility evident in his voice sent chills

scudding down the length of her spine. 'The hell you will.'

His features hardened, and a muscle tensed at the side of his jaw. 'Try to walk out of this apartment, and see how far you get.'

Aysha allowed her gaze to travel the length of his body, and back again. He had the height, the sheer strength to overcome any evasive tactics she might employ.

'Brute force, Carlo? Isn't that a little drastic?'

'Not when your well-being and safety are at stake.'

Her chin tilted in a gesture of defiance. 'Somehow that doesn't quite add up, does it?' She held up her hand as he began to speak. 'Don't.' Her eyes held a brilliant sheen that was a mixture of anger, pride, and pain. 'At least let there be honesty between us.'

'I have never been dishonest with you.'

She felt sick inside, a dreadful gnawing emptiness that ripped away any illusions she might have had that affection and caring on his part were enough.

Without a further word she turned and walked towards the front door, released the locking mechanism, then took the few steps necessary to reach the bank of lifts.

Please, *please* let there be one waiting, she silently begged as she depressed the call button.

The following twenty seconds were among the longest in her life, and she gave an audible sigh of relief when the heavy stainless steel doors slid open.

Aysha stepped inside and turned to jab the appropriate floor panel, only to gasp with outraged indignation as Carlo stepped into the cubicle.

'Get out.'

Dark eyes lanced hers, mercilessly hard and resolute. 'I can drive you, or follow behind in my car.' The ruthlessness intensified. 'Choose.'

The lift doors slid closed, and the cubicle moved swiftly down towards the car park.

'Go to hell.'

His smile held little humour. 'That wasn't an option.'

'Unfortunately.'

The flippant response served to tighten his expression into a grim mask, and his anger was a palpable entity.

'Believe you wouldn't want me to take you there.' His drawl held a silky threat that sent shivers scudding down the length of her spine.

The doors whispered open, and without a word she preceded him into the huge concrete cavern. Her car was parked next to his, and she widened the distance between them, conscious of her heels clicking against the concrete floor.

Carlo crossed to the Mercedes, unlocked the passenger door, and held it open. 'Get in.'

Damned if she'd obey his dictum. 'I'll need my car in the morning.'

His expression remained unchanged. 'I'll collect you.'

Aysha felt like stamping her foot. 'Or I can have Teresa drop me, or take a cab, or any one of a few other options.' Her eyes were fiery with rebellion. 'Don't patronise me, dammit!'

It had been a long night, fraught with moments of sheer anger, disillusionment, and introspective rationalisation. None of which had done much to ease the heartache or the sense of betrayal. Each of which she'd examined in detail, only to silently castigate herself for having too high an expectation of a union based solely in reality.

Worse, for allowing Nina's deviousness to undermine her own ambivalent emotions. Nina's success focused on Aysha's insecurity, and it irked unbearably.

Carlo watched the fleeting emotions chase across her expressive features and divined each and every one of them.

'Get in the car, *cara*.'

His gentle tone was almost her undoing, and she fought against the sudden prick of tears. Damn him. She wanted to maintain her anger. Lash out, verbally and physically, until the rage was spent.

Conversely, she needed his touch, the soothing quality of those strong hands softly brushing her skin, the feel of his mouth on hers as the sensual magic wove its own spell.

She wanted to re-enter the lift and have it transport them back to his apartment. Most of all, she wanted to lose herself in his loving, then fall asleep in his arms with the steady beat of his heart beneath her cheek.

Yet pride prevented her from taking that essential

step, just as it locked the voice in her throat. She felt raw, and emotionally at odds.

Did most brides suffer this awful ambivalence? *Get real*, a tiny voice reminded her. You don't represent *most* brides, and while you have the groom's affection, it's doubtful he'll ever gift you his unconditional love.

With a gesture indicating silent acquiescence she slid into the passenger seat, reached for the safety belt as Carlo closed the door, and fastened it as he crossed in front of the vehicle. Seconds later he fired the engine and cruised up the ramp leading to street level.

'Call your parents.'

Aysha reached into her purse and extracted the small mobile phone, and keyed in the appropriate digits.

Giuseppe answered on the third ring. 'Aysha? Something is wrong?'

'No, Papà. I'll be home in about fifteen minutes. Can you fix security?'

Thank heavens it wasn't Teresa who'd answered, for her mother would have fired off a string of questions to rival the Spanish Inquisition.

Aysha ignored Carlo's brief encompassing glance as the car whispered along the suburban street, and she closed her eyes against the image of her mother slipping on a robe in preparation for a maternal chat the instant Aysha entered the house.

A silent laugh rose and died in her throat. At this precise moment she didn't know which scenario she preferred... The emotive discussion she'd just had with Carlo, or the one she was about to have with Teresa.

Aysha had no sooner stepped inside the door than her mother launched into a series of questions, and it was easier to fabricate than spell out her own insecurities.

She justified her transgression by qualifying Teresa had enough on her plate, and nothing could be achieved by the confidence.

'Are you sure there is nothing bothering you?' Teresa persisted.

'No, Mamma.' Inspiration was the mother of invention, and she used it shamelessly. 'I forgot to take the samples I need to match up the shoes tomorrow, so I thought I'd come home.'

'You didn't quarrel with Carlo?'

Quarrel wasn't exactly the word she would have chosen to describe their altercation. 'Why would I do that?' Aysha countered.

'I'll make coffee.'

All she wanted to do was go to bed. 'Don't bother making it for me.'

'You're going upstairs now?'

'Goodnight, Mamma,' she bade gently. 'I'll see you in the morning.'

'Gianna and I will meet you for lunch tomorrow.' She mentioned a restaurant. 'I'll book a table for one o'clock.'

She leaned forward and brushed lips to her mother's cheek. 'That sounds nice.'

Without a further word she turned and made for the stairs, and in her room she slowly removed her clothes, cleansed her face of make-up, then slid in between the sheets.

CHAPTER FIVE

'I'LL be there in half an hour,' Carlo declared as Aysha took his call early next morning. 'Don't argue,' he added before she had a chance to say a word.

Conscious that Teresa sat within hearing distance as they shared breakfast she found it difficult to give anything other than a warm and friendly response.

'Thanks,' she managed brightly. 'I'll be ready.' She replaced the receiver, then drained the rest of her coffee. 'That was Carlo,' she relayed. 'I'll go change.'

'Will you come back here, or go straight into the city?'

'The city. I need to choose crockery and cutlery for the house.' Pots and pans, roasting dishes. Each day she tried to accumulate some of the necessities required in setting up house. 'I may as well make an early start.'

In her room, she quickly shed shorts and top and selected a smart straight skirt in ivory linen, added a silk print shirt and matching jacket, slid her feet into slim-heeled pumps, tended to her hair and make-up, and was downstairs waiting when Carlo's Mercedes slid to a halt outside the front door.

Aysha drew a calming breath, then she walked out to the car and slipped into the passenger seat. 'There was no need for you to collect me,' she assured him, conscious of the look of him, the faint aroma of his cologne.

'There was every need,' he drawled silkily as he sent the car forward.

'I don't want to fight with you,' she said ingenuously, and he spared her a swift glance.

'Then don't.'

A disbelieving laugh escaped her throat. 'Suddenly it doesn't seem that easy.'

'Nina is a woman who thrives on intrigue and innuendo.' Carlo's voice was hard, his expression an inscrutable mask.

Oh, yes, Aysha silently agreed. And she's so very good at it. 'She wants *you*.'

'I'm already spoken for, remember?'

'Ah, now there's the thing. Nina abides by the credo of *all being fair in love and war*.'

'And this is shaping up as war?'

You'd better believe it! 'You're the prize, *darling*,' she mocked, and incurred his dark glance.

'Yours.'

'You have no idea how gratifying it is to hear you say that.'

'Cynicism doesn't suit you.' Carlo slanted her a slight smile, and she raised one eyebrow in mocking acquiescence.

'Shall we change the subject?'

He negotiated an intersection, then turned into Rose Bay.

'I've booked a table for dinner tonight. I'll collect you at six.'

They'd had tickets for tonight's première performance by the Russian *corps de ballet* for a month. How could she not have remembered?

The remainder of the short drive was achieved in silence, and Carlo deposited her beside her car, then left as she slid in behind the wheel of the Porsche.

City traffic was horrific at this hour of the morning, and it was after nine when Aysha emerged onto the inner city street.

First stop was a major department store two blocks distant, and she'd walked less than half a block when her mobile phone rang.

She automatically retrieved the unit from her bag and heard Teresa's voice, pitched high in distress.

'Aysha? I've just had a call from the bridal boutique. Your headpiece has arrived from Paris, but it's the wrong one!'

She closed her eyes, then opened them again. It had taken a day of deliberation before making the final choice... How long ago? A month? Now the order had been mixed up. Great. 'OK, Mamma. Let's not panic.'

Her mother's voice escalated. 'It was perfect, just perfect. There wasn't another to compare with it.'

'I'll go sort it out.' A phone call from the boutique to the manufacturer in Paris, and the use of a courier service should see a successful result.

Aysha should have known it couldn't be that simple.

'I've already done that,' the boutique owner relayed. 'No joy, unfortunately. They don't have another in stock. The design is intricate, the seed pearls needed are held up heaven knows where, and the gist of it is, we need to choose something else.'

'OK, let's do it.' It took an hour to select, ascertain the order could be filled and couriered within the week.

'That's definite,' the vendeuse promised.

Now why didn't that reassure her? Possibly because she'd heard the same words before.

An hour later she had to concede there were diverse gremlins at work, for the white embroidered stockings ordered hadn't arrived. The lace suspender belt had, but it didn't match the garter belt, as it was supposed to do.

Teresa would consider it a catastrophe. Aysha merely drew in a deep breath, ascertained the order might be correctly filled in time, decided *might* wasn't good enough, and opted to select something else with a guaranteed delivery.

It was after midday when she collected the last carry-bag and added it to the collection she held in each hand. Shoes? Did she have time if she was to meet Teresa and Gianna at Double Bay for lunch at one? She could always phone and say she'd be ten or fifteen minutes late.

With that thought in mind she entered the Queen Victoria building and made her way towards the shoe shop.

It was a beautiful old building, historically preserved, and undoubtedly heritage-listed. Aysha loved the ambience, the blend of old and modern, and she admired a shop display as she rode the escalator to the first floor.

She'd only walked a few steps when an exquisite bracelet showcased in a jeweller's window caught her eye, and she paused to admire it. The gold links were of an unusual design, and each link held a half-carat diamond.

'I'm sure you'll only have to purr prettily in Carlo's ear, and he'll buy it for you.'

Aysha recognised the voice and turned slowly to face the young woman at her side. 'Nina,' she acknowledged with a polite smile, and watched as Nina's expression became positively feline.

She took in the numerous carry-bags and their various emblazoned logos. 'Been shopping?'

Aysha effected a faint shrug. 'A few things I needed to collect.'

'I was going to ring and invite you to share a coffee with me. Can you manage a few minutes now?'

The last thing she wanted was a tête-à-tête with Nina...with or without the coffee. 'I really don't have time. I'm meeting Teresa and Gianna for lunch.'

'In that case...' She slid open her attaché case, extracted a large square envelope and slipped it into one of Aysha's carry-bags. 'Have fun with these. I'm sure you'll find them enlightening.' Closing the case, she proffered a distinctly feline smile. '*Ciao*. See you tomorrow night at the sculpture exhibition.'

Given the social circle in which they both moved, their attendance at the same functions was inevitable. Aysha entertained the fleeting desire to give the evening exhibition a miss, then dismissed the idea. Bruno would never forgive their absence.

Aysha caught the time on one of the clocks featured in the jeweller's window, and hurriedly made for the bank of escalators.

Five minutes later she joined the flow of traffic and negotiated a series of one-way streets before hitting the main arterial one that would join with another leading to Double Bay.

Teresa and Gianna were already seated at a table when she entered the restaurant, and she greeted them both warmly, then sank into a chair.

'Shall we order?'

'You were able to sort everything out with the bridal boutique?'

It was easier to agree. Afterwards she could go into detail, but right now, here, she didn't want Teresa to launch into a long diatribe. 'Yes.'

'*Bene.*' Her mother paused sufficiently long for the waiter to take their order. 'You managed to collect everything?'

'Except shoes, and I'm sure I'll find something I like in one of the shops here.' Double Bay held a number of exclusive shops and boutiques. 'I'll have a look when we've finished lunch.'

It was almost two when they emerged onto the pavement, and Aysha left both women to complete their shopping while she tended to the last few items on her list.

A rueful smile played at the edges of her mouth. In a little over a weeek all the planning, the shopping, the organising…it would all be over. Life could begin to return to normal. She'd be Aysha Santangelo, mistress of her own home, with a husband's needs to care for.

Just thinking about those needs was enough to send warmth coursing through her veins, and put wickedly sensuous thoughts in her head.

During the next two hours she added to the number of carry-bags filling the boot of her car. The envelope Nina had slid into one of them drew her attention, and she pulled it free, examined it, then, curious as to its contents, she undid the flap.

Not papers, she discovered. Photographs. Several of them. She looked at the first, and saw a man and a woman embracing in the foyer of a hotel.

Not any man. Carlo. And the woman was Nina.

Aysha's insides twisted and began to churn as she put it aside and looked at the next one, depicting the exterior and name of a Melbourne hotel, the one where Carlo had stayed three weeks ago when he'd been there for a few days on business. Supposedly business, for the following shot showed Carlo and Nina entering a lift together.

Aysha's fingers shook as she kept flipping the photographs over, one by one. Nina and Carlo pausing outside a numbered door. About to embrace. Kissing.

The evidence was clear enough. Carlo was having an affair…with Nina.

Her legs suddenly felt boneless, and her limbs began to shake. How dared he abuse her trust, her love…everything she'd entrusted in him?

If he thought she'd condone a mistress, he had another think coming!

Anger rose like newly ignited flame, and she thrust

the photographs back into the envelope, closed the boot, then slid in behind the wheel of her car.

There were many ways to hurt someone, but betrayal was right up there. She wanted to march into his office and instigate a confrontation. *Now.*

Except she knew she'd yell, and say things it would be preferable for no one else to overhear.

Wait, an inner voice cautioned as she negotiated peak hour traffic travelling the main east suburban road leading towards Vaucluse.

The car in front braked suddenly, and only a split-second reaction saved her from running into the back of it.

All her fine anger erupted in a stream of language that was both graphic and unladylike. Horns blared in rapid succession, car doors slammed, and there were voices raised in conflict.

Traffic banked up behind her, and it was ten minutes before she could ease her car forward and slowly clear an intersection clogged with police car, ambulance, tow-truck.

Consequently it was after five when she parked the car out front of her parents' home, and she'd no sooner entered the house than Teresa called her into the kitchen.

'I'll be there in a few minutes,' Aysha responded. 'After I've taken everything up to my room.'

A momentary stay of execution, she reflected as she made her way up the curved staircase. The carry-bags could be unpacked later. The photographs were private, very private, and she tucked them beneath her pillow.

She took a few minutes to freshen up, then she retraced her steps to the foyer. The kitchen was redolent with the smell of herbs and garlic, and a small saucepan held simmering contents on the ceramic hotplate.

Teresa stood, spoon in hand, as she added a little wine, a little water, before turning to face her daughter.

'You didn't tell me what happened at the bridal boutique.'

Aysha relayed the details, then waited for her mother's anticipated reaction. She wasn't disappointed.

'Why weren't they couriered out? Why weren't we told before this there might be a problem? I'll never use that boutique again!'

'You won't have to,' Aysha said drily. 'Believe me, I've no intention of doing a repeat performance in this lifetime.'

'We should have used someone else.'

'As most of the bridal boutiques get all their supplies from the same source, I doubt it would have made a difference.'

'You don't know that,' Teresa responded sharply. 'I should have dealt with it myself. Can't they get anything right? Now we learn the wedding lingerie doesn't match.'

'I'm sure Carlo won't even notice.'

Teresa gave her a look which spoke volumes. 'It doesn't matter whether he notices or not. You'll know. *I'll* know. And so will everyone else when you lift your dress and he removes the garter.' The vol-

ume of her voice increased. 'We spent hours selecting each individual item. Now nothing matches.'

'Mother.' *Mother* was bad. Its use forewarned of
frazzled nerves, and a temper stretched close to
breaking point. 'Calm down.' One look at Teresa's
face was sufficient to tell a verbal explosion was imminent, and she took a deep breath and released it
slowly. 'I'm just as disappointed as you are, but we
have to be practical.' Assertiveness probably wasn't
a good option at this precise moment. 'I've already
chosen something I'm happy with and they've guaranteed delivery within days.'

'I'll check it out in the morning.'

'There's no need to do that.'

'Of course there is, Aysha.' Teresa was adamant.
'We've put a great deal of business their way.'

If she stayed another minute, she'd spit the dummy
and they'd have a full-scale row. 'I haven't got time
to discuss it now. I have to shower and change, and
meet Carlo in less than an hour.'

It was a cop-out, albeit a diplomatic one, she decided as she quickly ascended the stairs. Differences
of opinion were one thing. All-out war was another.
Teresa was *Teresa*, and she was unlikely to change.

Damn Nina and her Mission. She was a bitch of
the first order. Desperate, and dangerous.

The worst kind, Aysha determined viciously as she
stripped off her clothes and stepped beneath the cascade of water.

Five minutes later she emerged, wound a towel
around her slender curves and crossed into the bed-

room bent on selecting something mind-blowing to wear.

Dressed to kill. What a marvellous analogy, she decided. One look at her mirrored reflection revealed a slender young woman in a black beaded gown that was strapless, backless, with a hemline that fell to her ankles. A long chiffon scarf lay sprawled across the bed and she draped it round her neck so both ends trailed down her back.

Make-up was, she determined, a little overstated. Somehow it seemed appropriate. Warriors painted themselves before they went into battle, didn't they? And there would be a battle fought before the night was over. She could personally guarantee it.

Teresa was setting the table in the dining room. 'Mamma, I'm on my way.'

Was it something in her voice that caused her mother to cast her a sharp glance? When it came to maternal instincts, Teresa's were second to none. 'Have a good time.'

That was entirely debatable. Dinner à deux followed by an evening at the ballet had definitely lost its appeal. 'Thanks.'

Fifteen minutes later she garaged her car in the underground car park, then rode the lift to Carlo's apartment. The envelope containing the photographs was in her hand, and the portrayed images on celluloid almost scorched her fingers.

He opened the door within seconds, and she saw his pupils widen in gleaming male appreciation. A shaft of intense satisfaction flared, and she took in the immaculate cut of his dark suit, the startling white cotton shirt, the splendid tie.

The perfectly groomed, wildly attractive fiancé. Loving, too, she added a trifle viciously as he drew her close and nuzzled the sensitive curve of her neck.

The right touch, the expert moves. It was almost too much to expect him to be faithful as well. His love, she knew, would never be hers to have. But fidelity... That was something she intended to insist on.

'What's wrong?'

Add *intuitive*, Aysha accorded. At least some of his senses were on track. She moved back a step, away from the traitorous temptation of his arms. It would be far too easy to lean in against him and offer her mouth for his kiss. But then she'd kiss him back, and that wouldn't do at all.

'What makes you think that?' she queried with deliberate calm, and saw his eyes narrow.

'We've never played guessing games, and we're not going to start now.'

Games, subterfuge, deception. They were one and the same thing. 'Really?'

His expression sharpened, accentuating the broad facial bone structure with its strong angles and planes. 'Spit it out, Aysha. I'm listening.'

Aysha rang the tip of one fingernail along the edge of the envelope. Eyes like crystallised smoke burned with a fiery heat as she thrust the envelope at him. 'You've got it wrong. You talk. I get to listen.'

He caught the envelope, and a puzzled frown creased his forehead. 'What the hell is this about?'

'*Hell* is a pretty good description. Open the damned thing. I think you'll get the picture.' She certainly had!

His fingers freed the flap and she watched him carefully as he extracted the sheaf of photos and examined them one by one.

His expression barely altered, and she had to hand it to him... He had tremendous control. Somehow his icy discipline had more effect than anger.

'Illuminating, wouldn't you agree?'

His gaze speared hers, dark, dangerous and as hard as granite. 'Very.'

Her eyes held his fearlessly. 'I think I deserve an explanation.'

'I stayed in that hotel, and, yes, Nina was there. But without any prior knowledge or invitation on my part.'

How could she believe him when Nina continued to drip poison at every turn?

'That's it?' She was so cool it was a wonder the blood didn't freeze in her veins.

'As far as I'm concerned.'

'I guess Nina just happened to be standing outside your room?' She swept his features mercilessly. 'I don't buy it.'

'It happens to be the truth.' His voice was inflexible, and Aysha's eyes were fearless as she met his.

'I'm fully aware our impending marriage has its base in mutual convenience,' she stated with restrained anger. 'But I insist on your fidelity.'

Carlo's eyes narrowed and became chillingly

calm. There was a leashed stillness apparent she knew she'd be wise to heed.

Except she was past wisdom, beyond any form of rationale. Did he have any conception of what she'd felt like when she'd sighted those photos? It was as if the tip of a sword pierced her heart, poised there, then thrust in to the hilt.

'My fidelity isn't in question.'

'Isn't it?'

'Would you care to rephrase that?'

'Why?' Aysha countered baldly. 'What part didn't you understand?'

'I heard the words. It's the motive I find difficult to comprehend.'

With admirable detachment she raked his large frame from head to toe, and back again. 'It's simple. In this marriage, there's only room for two of us.' She was so angry, she felt she might self-destruct. 'There's no way I'll turn a blind eye to you having a mistress on the side.'

'Why would I want a mistress?' Carlo queried with icy calm.

Her eyes flashed, a brilliant translucent grey that had the clarity and purity of a rare pearl. 'To complement my presence in the marital bed?'

His gaze didn't waver, and she fought against being trapped by the depth, the intensity. It was almost hypnotic, and she had the most uncanny sensation he was intent on dispensing with the layers that guarded her soul, like a surgeon using a scalpel with delicate precision.

'Nina has done a hatchet job, hasn't she?' Carlo

offered in a voice that sounded like silk being razed by tempered steel. 'Sufficiently damaging, that any assurance I give you to the contrary will be viewed with scepticism?' He reached out a hand and caught hold of her chin between thumb and forefinger. 'What we share together,' he prompted. 'What would you call that?'

She was breaking up inside, slowly shattering into a thousand pieces. *Special*, a tiny voice taunted. So special, the mere thought of him sharing his body with someone else caused her physical pain.

'Good sex?' Carlo persisted dangerously.

Her stance altered slightly, and her eyes assumed a new depth and intensity. 'Presumably not good enough,' she declared bravely.

It was possible to see the anger build, and she watched with detached fascination as the fingers of each hand clenched into fists, watched the muscles bunch at the edge of his jaw, the slight flaring of nostrils, and the darkening of his eyes.

He uttered a husky oath, and she said with deliberate facetiousness, 'Flattery isn't appropriate.'

Something moved in the depths of his eyes. An emotion she didn't care to define.

'Nina,' Carlo vented emotively, 'has a lot to answer for.'

Didn't she just! 'On that, at least, we agree.'

'Let's get this quite clear,' he said with dangerous quietness. 'You have my vow of fidelity, just as I have yours. Understood?'

She wanted to lash out, then pick up something

and smash it. The satisfaction would be immensely gratifying.

'Aysha?' he prompted with deadly quietness, and she forced herself to respond.

'Even given that Nina is a first-class bitch, I find it a bit too much of a coincidence for you both to be in Melbourne at the same time, staying in the same hotel, the same floor.' Aysha drew in a deep breath. 'Photographic proof bears considerable weight, don't you think?'

He could have shaken her within an inch of her life. For having so little faith in him. So little trust.

'Did it not occur to you to consider it strange that a photographer just happened to be in the hotel lobby at the time Nina and I entered it…coincidentally together? Or that her suite and mine were very conveniently sited opposite each other?' It hadn't taken much pressure to discover Nina had bribed the booking receptionist to reshuffle bookings. 'Perhaps a little too convenient the same photographer was perfectly positioned to take a shot Nina had very carefully orchestrated?'

'You were kissing her!'

'Correction,' he drawled with deliberate cynicism. 'She was kissing me.'

Nina's words rose to the forefront of Aysha's mind. Vicious, damaging, and incredibly pervasive. 'Really? There didn't seem a marked degree of distinction to me.'

He extended his hands as if to catch hold of her shoulders, only to let them fall to his sides. 'A few seconds either way of that perfectly timed shot, and the truth would have been clearly evident.'

'According to Nina,' Aysha relayed bitterly, 'you represent the ultimate prize in the *most suitable husband* quest. Rich, handsome, and, as reputation has it...*a lover to die for.*' Her smile was a mere facsimile. 'Her words, not mine.'

Something fleeting darkened his eyes. A quality that was infinitely ruthless.

'An empty compliment, considering it's completely false.'

The celluloid print of that kiss rose up to haunt her. 'A willing, voluptuous female well-versed in every sexual trick in the book.' Her eyes swept his features, then focused on the unwavering depth of those dark eyes. 'You mean to say you refused what was so blatantly offered?' It took considerable effort to keep her voice steady. 'How noble.'

Carlo reached forward and caught hold of her chin, increasing the pressure as she attempted to twist out of his grasp.

'Why would I participate in a quick sexual coupling with a woman who means nothing to me?'

He was almost hurting her, and her eyes widened as he slid a hand to her nape and held it fast.

'A moment's aberration when your libido took precedence?' she sallied, hating the way his cologne teased her nostrils and began playing havoc with her equilibrium.

Oh, God, she didn't know anything any more. There were conflicting emotions warring inside her head, some of which hardly made any sense.

'Aysha?'

Her eyes searched his, wide, angry, and incredibly hurt. 'How would you feel if the situation were reversed?'

A muscle bunched at the side of his jaw, and something hot and terrifyingly ruthless darkened his eyes.

'I'd kill him.'

His voice was deadly quiet, yet it held the quality of tempered steel, and she felt as if a hand took hold of her throat and squeezed until it choked off her breath.

Her chest tightened and her heart seemed to beat loud, the sound a heavy, distant thud that seemed to reverberate inside her ears.

'A little extreme, surely?' Aysha managed after several long seconds.

'You think so?'

'That sort of action would get you long service, perhaps even life, in gaol.'

'Not for the sort of death I have in mind.' His features assumed a pitiless mask.

He had the power, the influence, to financially ruin an adversary. And he would do it without the slightest qualm.

A light shivery sensation feathered over the surface of her skin. She needed time out from all the madness that surrounded her. Somewhere she could gain solitude in which to think. A place where she had an element of choice.

'I'm going to move into the house for a few days.'

The words emerged almost of their own accord, and she saw his eyes narrow fractionally.

'It's the house, or a hotel,' Aysha insisted, meaning every word.

He wanted to shake her. Paramount was the desire to wring Nina's neck. Anger, frustration, irritation…each rose to the fore, and he banked them all down in an effort to conciliate.

'If that's what it takes.'

'Thank you.'

She was so icily polite, so remote. Pain twisted his gut, and he swore beneath his breath.

'We're due at the ballet in an hour.'

'Go alone, or don't go at all, Carlo. I really don't care.'

Aysha walked into the bedroom and caught up a few essentials from drawers, the wardrobe, aware that Carlo stood watching her every move from the doorway.

For one tragic second she felt adrift, homeless. Which was ridiculous. The thought made her angry, and she closed the holdall, then slung the strap over one shoulder.

'Aysha.'

She'd taken only a token assortment of clothing. That fact should have been reassuring, yet he'd never felt less assured in his life.

Clear grey eyes met his, unwavering in their clarity. 'Right now, there isn't a word you can say that will make a difference.'

She walked to the doorway, stepped past him, and made her way through the apartment to the front door. She half expected him to stop her, but he didn't.

The lift arrived swiftly, and she rode it down to the car park, unlocked her car, then drove it up onto the road.

Carlo leaned his back against the wall and stared sightlessly out of the wide plate-glass window. After a few tense minutes, he picked up the receiver, keyed in a series of digits, then waited for it to connect.

The private detective was one of the best, and with modern technology he should have the answer Carlo needed within days.

He made three more calls, offered an obscene amount of money to ensure that his requests... *orders*, he amended with grim cynicism, were met within a specified time-frame.

Now, he had to wait. And continue to endure Aysha's farcical pretence for a few days. Then there would be no more room for confusion.

He moved away from the wall, prowled the lounge, then in a restless movement he lifted a hand and raked fingers through his hair.

Yet strength wasn't the answer. Only proof, irrefutable proof.

In business, it was essential to cover all the bases, and provide back-up. He saw no reason why it wouldn't work in his personal life.

CHAPTER SIX

AYSHA was hardly aware of the night, the flash of headlights from nearby vehicles, as she traversed the streets and negotiated the Harbour Bridge. She handled the car with the movements of an automaton, and it was something of a minor miracle she reached suburban Clontarf.

Celestial guidance, she decided wryly as she activated the wrought-iron gates guarding entrance to the architectural masterpiece Carlo had built.

Remote-controlled lights sprang on as she reached the garage doors, and she checked the alarm system before entering the house.

It was so quiet, so still, and she crossed into the lounge to switch on the television, then cast a glance around the perfectly furnished room.

Beautiful home, luxuriously appointed, every detail perfect, she reflected; except for the relationship of the man and woman who were to due to inhabit it.

A weary sigh escaped her lips. Was she being foolish seeking a temporary escape? What, after all, was it going to achieve?

Damn. Damn Nina and the seeds she'd deliberately planted.

A slight shiver shook her slender frame, and she resolutely made her way to the linen closet. It was late, she was tired, and all she had to do was fetch fresh linen, make up the bed, and slip between the sheets.

She looked at the array of linen in their neat piles, and her fingers hovered, then shifted to a nearby stack.

Not the main bedroom. The bed was too large, and she couldn't face the thought of sleeping in it alone.

A guest bedroom? Heaven knew there were enough of them! She determinedly made her way towards the first of four, and within minutes she'd completed the task.

In a bid to court sleep she opted for a leisurely warm shower. Towelled dry, she caught up a cotton nightshirt and slid into bed to lie staring into the darkness as her mind swayed every which way but loose.

Carlo. Was he in bed, unable to sleep? Or had he opted to attend the ballet, after all?

What if Nina was also there? The wretched woman would be in her element when she discovered Carlo alone. Oh, for heaven's sake! Be sensible.

Except she didn't *feel* sensible. And sleep was never more distant.

Perhaps she did fall into a fitful doze, although it seemed as if she'd been awake all night when dawn filtered through the drapes and gradually lightened the room.

She lifted her left wrist and checked the time. A few minutes past six. There was no reason for her to rise this early, but she couldn't just lie in bed.

Aysha thrust aside the covers and padded barefoot

to the kitchen. The refrigerator held a half-empty bottle of fruit juice, a partly eaten sandwich, and an apple.

Not exactly required sustenance to jump-start the day, she decided wryly. So, she'd go shopping, stop off at a café for breakfast, then come back, change, and prepare to meet Teresa at ten. Meantime she'd try out the pool.

It was almost seven when she emerged, and she blotted off the excess moisture, then wrapped the towel sarong-wise and re-entered the house.

Within minutes the phone rang, and she reached for it automatically.

'You slept well?'

Aysha drew in a deep breath at the sound of that familiar voice. 'Did you expect me not to?'

There was a faint pause. 'Don't push it too far, *cara*,' Carlo drawled in husky warning.

'I'm trembling,' she evinced sweetly.

'So you should be.' His voice tightened, and acquired a depth that sent goosebumps scudding over the surface of her skin.

'Intimidation isn't on my list.'

'Nor is false accusation on mine.'

With just the slightest lack of care, this could easily digress into something they both might regret.

With considerable effort she banked down the anger, and aimed for politeness. 'Is there a purpose to your call, other than to enquire if I got any sleep?' She thought she managed quite well. 'I have a host of things to do.'

'*Grazie.*'

She winced at the intended sarcasm. *'Prego,'* she concluded graciously, and disconnected the phone.

On reflection, it wasn't the best of days, but nor was it the worst. Teresa was in fine form, and so consumed with her list of Things to Do, Aysha doubted her own preoccupation was even noticed. Which was just as well, for she couldn't have borne the string of inevitable questions her mother would deem it necessary to ask.

'You're looking a little peaky, darling. You're not coming down with something, are you?'

'A headache, Mamma.' It wasn't too far from the truth.

Teresa frowned with concern. 'Take some tablets, and get some rest.'

As if *rest* was the panacea for everything! 'Carlo and I are attending the sculpture exhibition at the Gallery tonight.'

'It's just as well Carlo is whisking you away to the Coast for the weekend. The break will do you good.'

Somehow Aysha doubted it.

The Gallery held a diverse mix of invited guests, some of whom attended solely to be seen and hopefully make the social pages. Others came to admire, with a view to adding to their collection.

Carlo and Aysha fell into a separate category. A close friend was one of the exhibiting artists and they wanted to add their support.

'Ciao, bella,' a male voice greeted, and Aysha

turned to face the extraordinarily handsome young man who'd sent his personal invitation.

'Bruno!' She flung her arms wide and gave him an enthusiastic hug. 'How are you?'

'The better for seeing you.' He lowered his head and bestowed a kiss to each cheek in turn. 'Damn Carlo for snaring you first.' He withdrew gently and looked deeply into those smoky grey eyes, then he turned towards Carlo and lifted one eyebrow in silent query. 'Carlo, *amici. Come stai?*'

Something passed between both men. Aysha glimpsed it, and sought to avert any swing in the territorial parameters by tucking one hand through Carlo's arm.

'Come show us your exhibits.'

For the next half-hour they wandered the large room, pausing to examine and comment, or converse with a few of the fellow guests.

Aysha moved towards a neighbouring exhibit as Carlo was temporarily waylaid by a business acquaintance.

'Your lips curve wide with a generous smile, yet your eyes are sad,' said Bruno. 'Why?'

'The wedding is a week tomorrow.' She gave a graceful shrug. 'Teresa and I have been shopping together every day, and nearly every night Carlo and I have been out.'

'Sad, *cara*,' Bruno reiterated. 'I didn't say tired. If Carlo isn't taking care of you, he will answer to me.'

She summoned a wicked smile and her eyes sparkled with hidden laughter. 'Swords at dawn? Or should that be pistols?'

'I would take pleasure in breaking his nose.'

She turned to check on the subject of their discussion, and stiffened. Bruno, acutely perceptive, shifted his head and followed her gaze. 'Ah, the infamous Nina.'

The statuesque brunette looked stunning in red, the soft material hugging every curve like a well-fitting glove.

Bruno leant down and said close to Aysha's ear, 'Shall we go break it up?'

'Let's do that.' The smile she proffered didn't reach her eyes, and her heart hammered a little in her chest as she drew close.

Nina's tapered red-lacquered nails rested on Carlo's forearm, and Aysha watched those nails conduct a gentle caressing movement back and forth over a small area of his tailored jacket.

Nina's make-up was superb, her mouth a perfect glossy red bow.

'Want me to charm her?' Bruno murmured, and Aysha responded equally quietly.

'Thanks, but I can fight my own battles.'

'Take care, *cara*. You're dealing with a dangerous cat.' He paused as they reached Carlo's side. 'Your most precious possession,' Bruno said lightly, and inclined his head with deliberate mockery, 'Nina.' Then he smiled, and moved through the crowd.

Wise man, Aysha accorded silently, wishing she could do the same.

'Darling, do get me a drink. You know what I like.'

Aysha began a mental countdown the moment Carlo left to find a waitress.

'I imagine you've checked the photographs?' Nina raised one eyebrow and raked Aysha's slender frame. 'Caused a little grief, did they?'

'Wasn't that your purpose?' Aysha was cold, despite the warmth of the summer evening.

'How clever of you,' Nina approved. 'Have you decided to condone his transgressions? I do hope so.' Her smile was seductively sultry. 'I would hate to have to give him up.'

Her heart felt as if it was encased in ice. 'You've missed your vocation,' she said steadily.

'What makes you say that, darling?'

She needed the might of a sword, but a verbal punch-line was better than nothing. 'You should have been an actress.' A smile cost her almost every resource she had, but she managed one beautifully, then she turned and threaded her way towards one of Bruno's sculptures.

'Who won?'

Bruno could always be counted on, and she cast him a wry smile. 'You noticed.'

'Ah, but I was looking out for you.' He curved an arm around the back of her waist. 'Now, tell me what you think about this piece.'

She examined it carefully. 'Interesting,' she conceded. 'If I say it resembles my idea of an African fertility god, would it offend you?'

'Not at all, because that's exactly what it is.'

'You're just saying that to make me feel good.'

He placed a hand over his heart. 'I swear.'

She began to laugh, and he smiled down at her. 'Why not me, *cara*?' he queried softly, and hugged her close. 'I'd treat you like the finest porcelain.'

'I know,' she said gently, and with a degree of very real regret.

'You love him, don't you?'

'Is it that obvious?'

'Only to me,' he assured her quietly. 'I just hope Carlo knows how fortunate he is to have you.'

'He does.'

Aysha heard that deep musing drawl, glimpsed the latent darkness in his eyes, and gently extricated herself from Bruno's grasp. 'I was admiring Bruno's sculpture.'

Carlo cast her a glittering look that set her nerves on edge. How dared he look at her like that when he'd been playing *up close and personal* with Nina?

'Don't play games, *cara*,' Carlo warned as soon as Bruno was out of earshot.

'Practise what you preach, *darling*,' she said sweetly. 'And *please* get me a drink. It'll give Nina another opportunity to waylay you.'

He bit off a husky oath. 'We can leave peaceably, or not,' he said with deceptive quietness. 'Your choice.' He meant every word.

'Bruno will be disappointed.'

'He'll get over it.'

'I could make a scene,' Aysha threatened, and his expression hardened.

'It wouldn't make any difference.'

It would, however, give Nina the utmost pleasure

to witness their dissension. 'I guess we get to say goodnight,' she capitulated with minimum grace.

Ten minutes later she was seated in the Mercedes as it purred across the Harbour Bridge towards suburban Clontarf.

She didn't utter a word during the drive, and she reached for the door-clasp the instant Carlo drew the car to a halt. It would be fruitless to tell him not to follow her indoors, so she didn't even try.

'Bruno is a friend. A good friend,' she qualified, enraged at his high-handedness. 'Which is more than I can say for Nina.'

'Neither Bruno nor Nina are an issue.'

Her chin tilted as she glared up at him. 'Then what the hell is the issue?'

'We are,' he vouchsafed succinctly.

'Well, now,' Aysha declared. 'There's the thing. Nina is quite happy for you to marry me, just as long as she gets to remain your mistress.'

His eyes filled with chilling intensity. 'Nina has one hell of an imagination.'

She'd had enough. 'Go home, Carlo.' Her eyes blazed with fury. 'If you don't, I'll be tempted to do something I might regret.'

She wasn't prepared for the restrained savagery evident as his mouth fastened on hers, forcing it open and controlling it as his tongue pillaged the inner sweetness. It was a deliberate ravishment of her senses. Claim-staking, punishing. She lost all sensation of time as one hand slid through her hair to hold fast her head, while the other curved low down her back.

Then the pressure eased, and the punishing quality changed to passion, gradually dissipating to a sensuous gentleness that curled round her inner core and tugged at her emotions, seducing until she was weak-willed and malleable.

From somewhere deep inside she dredged sufficient strength to tear her mouth free, and her body trembled as he traced the edge of his thumb across the swollen contours of her lips.

'Nina is nothing to me, do you understand? She never has been. Never will be.'

She didn't say a word. She just looked at him, glimpsed the faint edge of regret, and was incapable of moving.

He pulled her close and buried her head in the curve of his shoulder, then he pressed his lips to her hair.

Aysha could feel the power in that large body, the strength, and she felt strangely ambivalent. 'I don't want you to stay.'

'Because you'll only hate me in the morning?'

She drew a shaky breath. 'I'll hate myself even more.'

All he had to do was kiss her, and she'd change her mind. Part of her wanted him so much it was an impossible ache. Yet if she succumbed she'd be lost, and that wouldn't achieve a thing.

He held her for what seemed an age, then he turned her face to his and brushed his lips across her own, lingered at one corner and angled his mouth into hers in a kiss that was so incredibly evocative it dispensed with almost all her doubts.

Almost, but not quite. He sensed the faint barrier, and gently put her at arm's length.

'I'll pick you up at seven, OK?'

It was easy to simply nod her head, and she watched as he turned and walked to the door. Seconds later she heard his car's engine start, and she checked the lock, then activated security before crossing to her room.

Sleep seemed a distant entity, and she switched on the television in the hope of discovering something which would occupy her interest. Except channel-hopping provided nothing she wanted to watch, and she retired to her bedroom, then lay staring at the ceiling for what seemed hours before finally slipping into a restless slumber in which vivid dreams assumed nightmarish proportion as Nina took the role of vamp.

CHAPTER SEVEN

AYSHA woke early, padded barefoot to the kitchen, poured herself some fresh orange juice, then headed outdoors to swim several laps of the pool.

After fifteen minutes or so she emerged, towelled off the excess moisture, then retreated indoors to change and make breakfast.

The ambivalence of the previous evening had disappeared, and in the clear light of day it seemed advantageous for she and Carlo to spend the weekend apart.

With that thought in mind she crossed to the phone and punched in his number. The answering machine picked up, and she replaced the receiver down onto the handset.

He was probably in the shower, or, she determined with a glance at her watch, he could easily have left. She keyed in the digits that connected with his mobile, and got voicemail.

Damn. It would have been less confrontational to cancel via the phone than deal with him in person.

It was almost seven when Carlo walked into the kitchen, and his eyes narrowed at the sight of her in cut-off denims and skimpy top.

'You're not ready.'

'No.' Her response was matter-of-fact. 'I think we both need the weekend apart.'

His expression was implacable. 'I disagree. Go change and get your holdall. We don't have much time.'

'Give me one reason why I should go?' she demanded, tilting her chin at him in a way that drove him crazy, for he wanted to kiss her until all that fine anger melted into something he could deal with.

'I can give you several. But right now you're wasting valuable time.'

Without a word he strode through the lounge and ascended the stairs. She followed after him, watching as he entered the bedroom, opened a cupboard, extracted a leather holdall and tossed it down onto the bed, then he riffled through her clothes, selected, discarded, then opened drawers and took a handful of delicate underwear and dumped it in the holdall.

'What in hell do you think you're doing?'

A pair of heeled pumps followed sandals.

'I would have thought it was obvious.'

He moved into the *en suite* bathroom, collected toiletries and make-up, and swept them into a cosmetic case. He lifted his head long enough to spare her a searching look.

'You might want to change.'

Her eyes flashed fire. 'I might not,' she retaliated swiftly.

He shrugged his shoulders, pressed everything into the holdall, then closed the zip fastener.

'OK, let's go.'

'Don't you *listen*?' His implacability brought her to a state of rage. 'I am not going anywhere.'

Carlo was dangerously calm. Too calm. 'We've already done this scene.'

Aysha was too angry to apply any caution. 'Well, *hell*. Let's do it again.'

'No.' He slung the holdall straps over one shoulder, then he curved an arm round her waist and hoisted her over one shoulder with an ease that brought forth a gasp of outrage.

'You fiend! What do you think you're doing?'

'Abducting you.'

'In the name of God... *Why?*'

Carlo strode out of the room and began descending the short flight of stairs. 'Because we're flying to the Coast, as planned.'

She struggled, and made no impression. In sheer frustration she pummelled both hands against his back. 'Put me down!'

He didn't alter stride as he negotiated the stairs, and she aimed for his ribs, his kidneys, anywhere that might cause him pain. All to no avail, for he didn't so much as grunt when each punch connected.

'If you don't put me down this *instant*, I'll have you arrested for attempted kidnapping, assault, and anything else I can think of!'

Carlo reached the impressive foyer, took three more steps, then lowered her to stand in front of him.

'No, you won't.'

He was bigger, broader, taller than her, yet she refused to be intimidated. 'Want to bet?'

'Cool it, *cara*.'

'I am not your darling.'

His mouth curved with amusement, and she poked him several times in the chest.

'Don't you *dare* laugh!'

He curled his hands over her shoulders and held her still. 'What would you have me do? Kiss you? Haul you across one knee and spank your deliciously soft *derrière*?'

'Soft?' She worked out, and while her butt might be curved, it was tight.

'If you keep opposing me, I'll be driven to effect one or the other.'

'Lay a hand on me, and I'll—'

He was much too swift, and any further words she might have uttered were lost as his mouth closed over hers in a deep, punishing kiss which took hold of her anger and turned it into passion.

Aysha wasn't conscious when it changed, only that it did, and the fists she lashed him with gradually uncurled and crept up to his nape to cling as emotion wrought havoc and fragmented all her senses.

Carlo slowly eased the heat, and his mouth softened as he gently caressed the swollen contours of her lips, then pressed light butterfly kisses along the tender curve to one corner and back again.

When he lifted his head she could only look at him with drenched eyes, and he traced a forefinger down the slope of her nose.

'Now that I have your full attention... A weekend at the Coast will remove us from all the madness. No pressures, no demands, no social engagements.'

And no chance of accidentally bumping into Nina.

'Last call, Aysha,' Carlo indicated with a touch of mockery. 'Stay, or go. Which is it to be?'

It wasn't the time for deliberation. 'Go,' she said decisively, and heard his husky laughter.

They made the flight with ten minutes to spare, and touched down at Coolangatta Airport just over an hour later. It was almost ten when they checked into the hotel, and within minutes of entering into their suite Aysha crossed to the floor-to-ceiling glass window fronting the Broadwater, and released the sliding door.

She could hear the muted sound of traffic, voices drifting up from the pool area. Adjacent was an enclosed man-made beach with a secluded cave and waterfall.

In the distance she could see the architecturally designed roof resembling a collection of sails atop an exclusive shopping centre fronting a marina and connected by a walkway bridge to an exclusive ocean-front hotel.

A few minutes later she sensed rather than heard him move to stand behind her.

'Peaceful.'

It was, and she said so. 'Yes.'

His arms curved round her waist and he pulled her close. 'What do you want to do with the day?'

There was a desperate need to get out of the hotel suite, and lose herself among the crowds. 'A theme park?' She said the first one that came into her head. 'Dreamworld.'

He hid a wry smile. 'I'll organise it.'

'Just like that?'

'We can hire a car and drive into the mountains, take any one of several cruises.' His shoulders shifted as he effected a lazy shrug. 'You get to choose.'

'For today?'

'All weekend,' he said solemnly.

'Give me too much power, and it might go to my head,' Aysha teased, suddenly feeling more in control.

'I doubt it.'

He knew her too well. 'After dinner we go to the Casino, then tomorrow we do Movieworld.' Crowds, lots of people. Which left only the hours between midnight or later and dawn spent in this beautiful suite, with its very large, prominently positioned bed.

Dreamworld was fun. They played tourist and took a bus there, went on several rides, ate hot dogs and chips as they wandered among the crowd. Aysha laughed at the white tigers' antics, viewed the Tower of Terror and voiced an emphatic *no* to Carlo's suggestion they take the ride.

It was almost six when the bus deposited them outside the hotel.

'I'll have first take on the shower,' Aysha indicated as they rode the lift to their designated floor.

'We could share.'

'I don't think that's a good idea,' she said evenly. Just remembering how many showers they'd shared and their inevitable outcome set all her fine body hairs on edge.

The lift slid to a stop and she turned in the direction of their suite.

Inside, she collected fresh underwear and entered

the large bathroom. The water was warm and she adjusted the dial, undressed, then stepped into the tiled stall.

Seconds later the door slid open and her eyes widened as Carlo joined her.

'What do you think you're doing?'

'Sharing a shower isn't necessarily an invitation to have sex,' he said calmly, and took the soap from her nerveless fingers.

He was too close, but there was no further room to move.

'Want me to shampoo your hair?'

'I can do it,' she managed in a muffled voice, and she missed his slight smile as he uncapped the courtesy bottle and slowly worked the gel into her hair.

His fingers began a gentle massage, and she closed her eyes, taking care to stifle a despairing groan as he rinsed off the foam.

Not content, he palmed the soap and proceeded to smooth it over her back, her buttocks, thighs, before tending to her breasts, then her stomach.

'Don't,' Aysha begged as he travelled lower, and she shook her head in mute denial when he placed the soap in her hand, then guided it over his chest.

Her fingers scraped the curling hair there, and she felt the tautness of his stomach, then consciously held her breath as he'd traversed lower.

His arousal was a potent force, and she began to shake with the need for his possession. It would be so easy to let the soap slip from her hand and reach for him. To lift her face to his, and invite his mouth down to hers.

Then he turned and his voice emerged as a silky drawl. 'Do my back, *cara.*'

She thrust the soap onto its stand, and slid open the door. 'Do it yourself.'

Aysha escaped, only because he let her, she was sure, and she caught up a towel, clutched hold of her underwear, and moved into the bedroom.

It was galling to discover her hands were trembling, and she quickly towelled herself dry, then wound the towel turban-wise round her head.

By the time Carlo emerged she was dressed, and she re-entered the bathroom to utilise the hairdrier, then tend to her make-up.

White silk evening trousers, a gold-patterned white top, minimum jewellery, and white strapped heeled pumps made for a matching outfit.

Black trousers and a white chambray shirt emphasised his dark hair and tanned skin. He'd shaved, and his cologne teased her nostrils, creating a havoc all its own with her senses.

'Ready?'

They caught a taxi to the Casino, enjoyed a leisurely meal, then entered the gambling area.

Aysha's luck ran fickle, while Carlo's held, but she refused to use his accumulated winnings, choosing instead to watch him at the blackjack table. Each selection was calculated, his expression impossible to read. Much like the man himself, she acknowledged silently.

It was after one when they returned to the hotel. Aysha felt pleasantly tired, and in their suite she slipped out of her clothes, cleansed her face of make-up, then slid into bed to lie quietly with her eyes closed, pretending sleep.

Moments later she felt the mattress depress as Carlo joined her, and she measured her breathing into a slow, steady rise and fall. Grateful, she told herself, that Carlo's breathing gradually acquired a similar pattern.

Why was it that when you didn't want something, you felt cheated when you didn't receive it? Aysha queried silently. The size of the bed precluded any chance of accidentally touching, and she didn't feel inclined to instigate the contrived kind...

'Come on, sleepyhead, rise and shine.'

Aysha heard the voice and opened her eyes to brilliant sunshine and the aroma of freshly brewed coffee. It was *morning* already?

'Breakfast,' Carlo announced. 'You have three quarters of an hour to eat, shower and dress before we need to take the bus to Movieworld.'

What had happened to the night? You slept right through it, a tiny voice taunted. Wasn't that what you wanted?

They boarded the bus with a few minutes to spare, and there were thrills and spills and fun and laughter as the actors went through their paces. The various stuntmen and women earned Aysha's respect and admiration as more than once a scene made her catch her breath in awe of the sensitive degree of timing and expertise involved.

They caught the early evening-flight out of Coolangatta Airport, and arrived in Sydney after nine. Carlo collected the car, then headed towards the city.

For one brief moment Aysha was tempted to choose the apartment, except Carlo pre-empted any decision by driving to Clontarf.

She told herself fiercely that she wasn't disappointed as he checked the house and re-set the alarm.

His kiss was brief, a soft butterfly caress that left her aching for more. Then he turned and retraced his steps to the car.

Half an hour later Carlo crossed to the phone and punched in a series of digits, within minutes of entering his apartment.

Samuel Sloane, a legal eagle of some note, picked up on the seventh ring, and almost winced at the grim tone of the man who'd chosen to call him at such an hour on a Sunday evening at home. He listened, counselled and advised, and wasn't in the least surprised when he was ignored.

'I don't give a damn for the what-if's and maybes protecting my investments, my interests. I'm not consulting you for advice. I'm instructing you what to do. Draw up that document. I'll be in your office just before five tomorrow. Now, do we understand each other?'

The impulse to slam the receiver down onto the handset was uppermost, and Carlo barely avoided the temptation to do so.

Aysha spent the morning organising the final soft furnishing items she'd ordered several weeks previously. A message alerting her of their arrival had been on her answering machine when she'd checked it on her return from the Coast.

At midday she stood back and surveyed the results, and was well pleased with the effect. It was perfect, and just as she'd envisaged the overall look.

It was amazing how a few cushions, draped pelmets in matching fabric really set the final touch to a room.

All it needed, she decided with a critical eye, was a superbly fashioned terracotta urn in one corner to complete the image she wanted. Maybe she'd have time to locate the urn before she was due to meet Teresa at one.

Aysha made it with minutes to spare, and together they spent the next few hours with the dressmaker, checked a few minor details with the wedding organiser, then took time to relax over coffee.

'You haven't forgotten we're dining with Gianna and Luigi tonight?'

Aysha uttered a silent scream in sheer frustration. She didn't want to play the part of soon-to-be-married adoring fiancée. Nor did she want to dine beneath the watchful eyes of their respective parents.

When she arrived at the house she checked the answering machine and discovered a message from Carlo indicating he'd collect her at six. An identical message was recorded on her mobile phone.

Her fingers hovered over the telephone handset as she contemplated returning his call and cancelling out, only to retreat in the knowledge that she had no choice but to see the evening through.

A shower did little to ease the tension, and she

deliberately chose black silk evening trousers and matching halter-necked top, added stiletto pumps, twisted her hair into a simple knot atop her head, and kept make-up to a minimum.

She was ready when security alerted her that the front gate had been activated, and she opened the front door seconds ahead of Carlo's arrival.

He was a superb male animal, she conceded as she caught her first glimpse of him. Tall, broad frame, honed musculature, and he exuded a primitive alchemy that was positively lethal.

Expensively tailored black trousers, dark blue shirt left unbuttoned at the neck, and a black jacket lent a sophistication she could only admire. 'Shall we leave?' Aysha asked coolly, and saw those dark eyes narrow.

'Not yet.'

Her stomach executed a slow somersault, and she tensed involuntarily. 'We don't want to be late.'

He was standing too close, and she suppressed the need to take a backward step. She didn't need him close. It just made it more difficult to maintain a mental distance. And she needed to, badly.

He brushed his fingers across one cheek and pressed a thumb to the corner of her mouth. 'You're pale.'

She almost swayed towards him, drawn as if by a magnetic force. Dammit, how could she love him, yet hate him at the same time? It was almost as if her body was detached from the dictates of her brain.

'A headache,' she responded evenly, and his expression became intensely watchful.

'I'll ring and cancel.'

It was easier to handle him when he was angry. At least then she could rage in return. Now, she merely felt helpless, and it irked her that he knew.

'That isn't an option, and you know it,' she refuted, and lifted a hand in expressive negation.

'You've taken something for it?'

'Yes.'

'Povera piccola,' he declared gently as he lowered his head and brushed his lips against her temple.

Sensation curled inside her stomach as his mouth trailed down to the edge of her mouth, and she turned her head slightly, her lips parting in denial, only to have his mouth close over hers.

He caught her head between both hands, and his tongue explored the inner tissues at will, savouring the sweetness with such erotic sensuousness that all rational thought temporarily fled.

His touch was sheer magic, exotic, intoxicating, and left her wanting more. Much more.

It's just a kiss, she assured herself mentally, and knew she was wrong. This was seductive claim-staking at its most dangerous.

Aysha pushed against his shoulders and tore her mouth from his, her eyes wide and luminous as they caught the darkness reflected in his. Her mouth tingled, and her lips felt slightly swollen.

'Let's go.' Was that her voice? It sounded husky, and her mouth shook slightly as she moved away from him and caught up her evening bag.

In the car she leaned her head back against the

cushioned rest, and stared sightlessly out of the window.

Summer daylight saving meant warm sunshine at six in the evening, and peak-hour traffic crossing the Harbour Bridge had diminished, ensuring a relatively smooth drive to suburban Vaucluse.

Aysha didn't offer anything by way of conversation, and she was somewhat relieved when Carlo brought the Mercedes to a halt behind Teresa and Giuseppe's car in the driveway of his parents' home.

'Showtime.'

'Don't overdo it, *cara*,' he warned quizzically, and she offered him a particularly direct look.

Did he know just how much she hurt deep inside? Somehow she doubted it. 'Don't patronise me.'

She saw one eyebrow lift. 'Not guilty,' Carlo responded, then added drily, 'on any count.'

Now there was a *double entendre* if ever there was one. 'You underestimate yourself.'

His eyes hardened fractionally. 'Take care, Aysha.'

She reached for the door-clasp. 'If we stay here much longer, our parents will think we're arguing.'

'And we're not?'

'Now you're being facetious.' She opened the door and stood to her feet, then summoned a warm smile as he crossed to her side.

Gianna Santangelo's affectionate greeting did much to soothe Aysha's unsettled nerves. This was *family*, although she was under no illusions, and knew that both mothers were attuned to the slightest nuance that might give hint to any dissension.

Dinner was an informal meal, although Gianna had gone to considerable trouble, preparing *gnocchi* in a delicious sauce, followed by chicken pieces roasted in wine with rosemary herbs and accompanied by a variety of vegetables.

Gianna was a superb cook, with many speciality dishes in her culinary repertoire. Even Teresa had the grace to offer a genuine compliment.

'*Buona*, Gianna. You have a flair for *gnocchi* that is unsurpassed by anyone I know.'

'*Grazie*. I shall give Aysha the recipe.'

Ah, now there was the thing. Teresa's recipe versus that of Gianna. Tricky, Aysha concluded. Very tricky. She'd have to vary the sauce accordingly whenever either or both sets of parents came to dinner. Or perhaps not serve it at all? Maybe she could initiate a whole new range of Italian cuisine? Or select a provincial dish that differed from Trevisian specialities?

'I won't have time for much preparation except at the weekends.' She knew it was a foolish statement the moment the words left her mouth, as both Teresa and Gianna's heads rose in unison, although it was her mother who voiced the query.

'Why ever not, *cara*?'

Aysha took a sip of wine, then replaced her glass down onto the table. 'Because I'll be at work, Mamma.'

'But you have finished work.'

'I'm taking a six-week break, then I'll be going back.'

'Part-time, of course.'

'Full-time.'

Teresa stated the obvious. 'There is no need for you to work at all. What happens when you fall pregnant?'

'I don't plan on having children for a few years.'

Teresa turned towards Carlo. 'You agree with this?'

It could have been a major scandal they were discussing, not a personal decision belonging to two people.

'It's Aysha's choice.' He turned to look at her, his smile infinitely warm and sensual as he took hold of her hand and brushed his lips to each finger in turn. His eyes gleamed with sensual promise. 'We both want a large family.'

Bastard, she fumed silently. He'd really set the cat among the pigeons now. Teresa wouldn't be able to leave it alone, and she'd receive endless lectures about caring for a husband's needs, maintaining an immaculate house, an excellent table.

Aysha leaned forward, and traced the vertical crease slashing Carlo's cheek. His eyes flared, but she ignored the warning gleam. 'Cute, plump little dark-haired boys,' she teased as her own eyes danced with silent laughter. 'I've seen your baby pictures, remember?'

'Don't forget I babysat you and changed your nappies, *cara*.'

Her first memory of Carlo was herself as a four-year-old being carried round on his shoulders, laughing and squealing as she gripped hold of his hair for

dear life. She'd loved him then with the innocence
of a child.

Adoration, admiration, respect had undergone a
subtle change in those early teenage years, as raging
female hormones had labelled intense desire as sexual attraction, infatuation, lust.

He'd been her best friend, confidant, big brother,
all rolled into one. Then he'd become another girl's
husband, and it had broken her heart.

Now she was going to marry him, have his children, and to all intents and purposes live the fairy
tale dream of happy-ever-after.

Except she didn't have his heart. That belonged to
Bianca, who lay buried beneath an elaborate bed of
marble high on a hill outside the country town in
which she'd been born.

Aysha had wanted to hate her, but she couldn't,
for Bianca had been one of those rare human beings
who was so genuinely kind, so *nice*, she was impossible to dislike.

Carlo caught each fleeting expression and correctly
divined every one of them. His mouth softened as he
leant forward and brushed his lips to her temple.

She blinked rapidly, and forced herself to smile.
'Hands-on practice, huh? You do know you're going
to have to help with the diapering?'

'I wouldn't miss it for the world.'

Aysha almost believed him.

'I'll serve the *cannoli*,' Gianna declared. 'And afterwards we have coffee.'

'You women have the *cannoli*,' Luigi dismissed
with the wave of one hand. 'Giuseppe, come with

me. We'll have a brandy. With the coffee, we'll have *grappa*.' He turned towards his son. 'Carlo?'

Women had their work to do, and it was work which didn't involve men. Old traditions died hard, and the further they lived away from the Old Country, Aysha recognised ruefully, the longer it took those traditions to die.

Carlo rose to his feet and followed the two older men from the room.

Aysha braced herself for the moment Teresa would pounce. Gianna, she knew, would be more circumspect.

'You cannot be serious about returning to work after the honeymoon.'

Ten seconds. She knew, because she'd counted them off. 'I enjoy working, Mamma. I'm very good at what I do.'

'Indeed,' Gianna complimented her. 'You've done a wonderful job with the house.'

'*Ecco*,' Teresa agreed, and Aysha tried to control a silent sigh.

Her mother invariably lapsed into Italian whenever she became passionate about something. Aysha sank back in her chair and prepared for a lengthy harangue.

She wasn't disappointed. The use of Italian became more frequent, as if needed to emphasise a point. And even Gianna's gentle intervention did little to stem the flow.

'If you had to work, I could understand,' Teresa concluded. 'But you don't. There are hundreds, thousands,' she corrected, 'without work, and taking money from the government.'

Aysha gave a mental groan. Politics. They were in for the long haul. She cast a pleading glance at Carlo's mother, and received a philosophical shrug in response.

'I'll make coffee,' Gianna declared, and Aysha stood to her feet with alacrity.

'I'll help with the dishes.'

It was only a momentary diversion, for the debate merely shifted location from the dining room to the kitchen.

Aysha's head began to throb.

'Zia Natalina has finished crocheting all the baskets needed for the *bomboniera*,' Gianna interceded in a bid to change the subject. 'Tomorrow she'll count out all the sugared almonds and tie them into tulle circles. Her daughter Giovanna will bring them to the house early on the day of the wedding.'

'*Grazie*, Gianna. I want to place them on the tables myself.'

'Giovanna and I can do it, if it will help. You will have so much more to do.'

Teresa inclined her head. 'Carlo has the wedding rings? Annalisa has sewn the ring pillow, but the rings need to be tied onto it.' A frown furrowed her brow. 'I must phone and see if she has the ribbon ready.' She gathered cups and saucers together onto the tray while Gianna set some almond biscuits onto a plate.

'The men won't touch them, but if I don't put a plate down with something Luigi will complain.' She lifted a hand and let it fall to her side. 'Yet when I produce it, he'll say they don't want biscuits with coffee.' Her humour was wry. 'Men. Who can understand them?' She cast a practised eye over the tray. 'We have everything. Let's join them, shall we?'

All three men were grouped together in front of the television engrossed in a televised, soccer match.

Luigi was intent on berating the goal keeper for presumably missing the ball, Aysha determined, and her father appeared equally irate.

'Turn off the set,' Gianna instructed Luigi as she placed the tray down onto a coffee table. 'We have guests.'

'Nonsense,' he grumbled. 'They're family, not guests.'

'It is impossible to talk with you yelling at the players.' She cast him a stern glance. 'Besides, you are taping it. When you replay you can yell all you like. Now we sit down and have coffee.'

'*La moglie.*' He raised his eyes heavenward.

'*Dio madonna.* A man is not boss in his own house any more?'

It was a familiar by-play, and one Aysha had heard many times over the years. Her father played a similar verbal game whenever Gianna and Luigi visited.

Her eyes sought Carlo's, and she glimpsed the faint humorous gleam evident as they waited silently for Gianna to take up the figurative ball.

'Of course you are the boss. You need me to tell you this?'

Luigi cast the tray an accusing glance. 'You

brought biscuits? What for? We don't need biscuits with coffee. It spoils the taste of the *grappa*.'

'Teresa and Aysha don't have *grappa*,' she admonished. 'You don't think maybe we might like biscuits?'

'After *cannoli* you eat biscuits? You won't sleep with indigestion.'

'I won't sleep anyway. After *grappa* you snore.'

'I don't snore.'

'How do you know? Do you listen to yourself?'

Luigi spread his hands in an expansive gesture. 'Ah, *Mamma*, give it up, huh? We are with friends. You cooked a good dinner. Now it is time to relax.' He held out a beckoning hand to Aysha. 'Come here, *ma tesora*.'

She crossed to his side and rested against the arm he curved round her waist.

'When are you going to invite us to dinner at the new house?'

'After they get back from the honeymoon,' Gianna declared firmly. 'Not before. It will bring bad luck.'

Luigi didn't take any notice. 'Soon there will be *bambini*. Maybe already there is one started, huh, and you didn't tell us?'

'You talk too much,' his wife chastised. 'Didn't you hear Aysha say she intends to wait a couple of years? Aysha, don't listen to him.'

'Ah, grandchildren. You have a boy first, to kick the soccer ball. Then a girl. The brother can look after his sister.'

'Two boys,' Giuseppe insisted, joining the conversation. 'Then they can play together.'

'Girls,' Aysha declared solemnly. 'They're smarter, and besides they get to help me in the house.'

'A boy and a girl.'

'If you two *vecchios* have finished planning our children,' Carlo intruded mildly as he extricated Aysha from his father's clasp. 'I'm going to take Aysha home.'

'*Vecchios*? You call us old men?' Giuseppe demanded, a split second ahead of Luigi's query,

'What are you doing going home? It's early.'

'Why do you think they're going home?' Gianna disputed. 'They're young. They want to make love.'

'Perhaps we should fool them and stay,' Aysha suggested in an audible aside, and Carlo shook his head.

'It wouldn't make any difference.'

'But I haven't had my coffee.'

'You don't need the caffeine.'

'Making decisions for me?'

'Looking out for you,' Carlo corrected gently. 'A few hours ago you had a headache. Unless I'm wrong, you're still nursing one.'

So he deserved full marks for observation. Without a further word she turned towards Luigi and pressed a soft kiss to his cheek, then she followed suit with her father before crossing to Teresa and Gianna.

Saying goodbye stretched out to ten minutes, then they made it to the car, and seconds later Carlo eased the Mercedes through the gates and out onto the road.

CHAPTER EIGHT

'YOU threw me to the lions.'

'Wrong century, *cara*,' he informed her wryly. 'And the so-called lions are pussy cats at heart.'

'Teresa doesn't always sheath her claws.' It was an observation, not a condemnation. 'There are occasions when being the only chick in the nest is a tremendous burden.'

'Only if you allow it to be.'

The headache seemed to intensify, and she closed her eyes. 'Intent on playing amateur psychologist, Carlo?'

'Friend.'

Ah, now there's a descriptive allocation, Aysha reflected. *Friend*. It had a affectionate feel to it, but affection was a poor substitute for love. The all-encompassing kind that prompted men to kill and die for it.

She lapsed into silence as the car headed down towards Double Bay.

'How's the headache?'

It had become a persistent ache behind one eye that held the promise of flaring into a migraine unless she took painkillers very soon. 'There,' she informed succinctly, and closed her eyes against the glare of oncoming headlights.

Carlo didn't offer another word during the drive

to Clontarf, for which she was grateful, and she reached for the door-clasp as soon as the car drew to a halt outside the main entrance to the house.

Aysha turned to thank him, only to have the words die in her throat at his bleak expression.

'Don't even think about uttering a word,' he warned.

'Don't tell me,' she dismissed wearily. 'You're intent on playing nurse.'

His silence was an eloquent testament of his intention, and she slid from the car and mounted the few steps to the front door.

Within minutes he'd located painkillers and was handing them to her together with a tumbler of water.

'Take them.'

She swallowed both tablets, then spared him a dark glance. 'Yessir.'

'Don't be sassy,' he said gently.

Damn him. She didn't need for him to be considerate. Macho she could handle. His gentleness simply undid her completely.

Aysha knew she should object as he took hold of her hand and led her to one of the cushioned sofas, then pulled her down onto his lap, but it felt so *good* her murmur of protest never found voice.

Just close your eyes and enjoy, a tiny imp prompted.

It would take ten minutes for the tablets to begin to work, and when they did she'd get to her feet, thank him, see him out of the door, then lock up and go to bed.

In a gesture of temporary capitulation she tucked

her head into the curve of his neck and rested her cheek against his chest. His arms tightened fractionally, and she listened to the steady beat of his heart.

She'd lain against him like this many times before. As a young child, friend, then as a lover.

Memories ran like a Technicolor film through her head. A fall and scraped knees as a first-grade kid in school. When she'd excelled at ballet, achieved first place at a piano recital. But nothing compared with the intimacy they'd shared for the past three months. That was truly magical. So mesmeric it had no equal.

She felt the drift of his lips against her hair, and her breathing deepened to a steady rise and fall.

When Aysha woke daylight was filtering into the room.

The main bedroom. And she was lying on one side of the queen-size bed; the bedcovers were thrown back on the other. She conducted a quick investigation, and discovered all that separated her from complete nudity was a pair of lacy briefs.

Memory was instant, and she blinked slowly, aware that the last remnants of her headache had disappeared.

The bedroom door opened and Carlo's tall frame filled the aperture. 'You're awake.' His eyes met hers, their expression inscrutable. 'Headache gone?'

'You stayed.' Was that her voice? It sounded breathless and vaguely unsteady.

He looked as if he'd just come from the shower. His hair was tousled and damp, and a towel was hitched at his waist.

'You were reluctant to let me go.'

Oh, God. Her eyes flew to the pillow next to her own, then swept to meet his steady gaze. Her lips parted, then closed again. Had they…? No, of course they hadn't. She'd remember…wouldn't she?

'Carlo—'

Her voice died in her throat as he discarded the towel and pulled on briefs, then thrust on a pair of trousers and slid home the zip.

Each movement was highlighted by smooth rippling muscle and sinew, and she watched wordlessly as he shrugged his arms into a cotton shirt and fastened the buttons.

He looked up and caught her watching him. His mouth curved into a smile, and his eyes were warm, much too warm for someone she'd chosen to be at odds with.

'Mind if I use a comb?'

Her lips parted, but no sound came out, and with a defenceless gesture she indicated the *en suite* bathroom. 'Go ahead.'

She followed his passage as he crossed the room, and she conducted a frantic visual search for something to cover herself with so she could make it to the walk-in wardrobe.

Carlo emerged into the bedroom as she was about to toss aside the bedcovers, and she hastily pulled them up again.

'I'll make coffee,' he indicated. 'And start breakfast. Ten minutes?'

'Yes. Thanks,' she added, and wondered at her faint edge of disappointment as he closed the door behind him.

What had she expected? That he'd cross to the bed and attempt to kiss her? *Seduce* her?

Yet there was a part of her that wanted him to…badly.

With a hollow groan she tossed aside the covers and made for the shower.

Ten minutes later she entered the kitchen to the aroma of freshly brewed coffee. Carlo was in the process of sliding eggs onto a plate, and there were slices of toasted bread freshly popped and ready for buttering.

'Mmm,' she murmured appreciatively. 'You're good at this.'

'Getting breakfast?'

Dressed, she could cope with him. 'Among other things,' she conceded, and crossed to the coffee-maker.

Black, strong, with two sugars. There was nothing better to kick-start the day. 'Shall I pour yours?'

'Please.' He took both plates and placed them on the servery. 'Now, come and eat.'

Aysha took a seat on one of four bar stools and looked at the food on her plate. 'You've given me too much.'

'Eat,' bade Carlo firmly.

'You're as bad as Teresa.'

He reached out a hand and captured her chin. 'No,' he refuted, turning her head towards him. 'I'm not.'

His kiss was sensuously soft and incredibly sensual, and she experienced real regret when he gently put her at arm's length.

'I have to leave. Don't forget we're attending the

Zachariahs' party tonight. I'll call through the day and let you know a time.'

With only days until the wedding, the pressure was beginning to build. Teresa seemed to discover a host of last-minute things that needed organising, and by the end of the day she began to feel as if the weekend at the Coast had been a figment of her imagination.

The need to feel supremely confident was essential, and Aysha chose a long, slim-fitting black gown with a sheer lace overlay. The scooped neckline and ribbon shoulder straps displayed her lightly tanned skin to advantage, and she added minimum jewellery: a slender gold chain, a single gold bangle on one wrist, and delicate drop earrings. Stiletto-heeled evening pumps completed the outfit, and she spared her reflection a cursory glance.

Black was a classic colour, the style seasonally fashionable. She looked OK. And if anyone noticed the faint circles beneath her eyes, she had every excuse for their existence. A bride-to-be was expected to look slightly frazzled with the surfeit of social obligations prior to the wedding.

Carlo's recorded message on the answering machine had specified he'd collect her at seven-thirty. The party they were to attend was at Palm Beach, almost an hour's drive from Vaucluse, depending on traffic.

She would have given anything not to go. The thought of mixing and mingling with numerous social friends and acquaintances didn't appeal any more than having to put on an act for their benefit.

Security beeped as Carlo used the remote module

to release the gates, and Aysha's stomach executed a series of somersaults as she collected her evening purse and made her way down to the lower floor.

She opened the front door as he alighted from the car, and she crossed quickly down the few steps and slid into the passenger seat.

His scrutiny was swift as he slid in behind the wheel, encompassing, and she wondered if he was able to define just how much effort it cost her to appear cool and serene.

Inside, her nerves were stretched taut, and she felt like a marionette whose body movements were governed by a disembodied manipulator.

She met his dark gaze with clear distant grey eyes. No small acting feat, when her body warmed of its own accord, heating at the sight of him and his close proximity.

His elusive cologne invaded her senses, stimulating them into active life, and every nerve-end, every fibre seemed to throb with need.

The *wanting* didn't get any better. If anything, each passing hour made it worse. Especially the long, empty nights when she hungered for his touch.

'How are you?'

Three words spoken in a commonplace greeting, yet they had the power to twist Aysha's stomach into a painful knot.

'Fine.' She didn't aim to tell him anything different.

Carlo eased the car forward, past the gates, then he accelerated along the suburban street with controlled ease.

She directed her attention beyond the windscreen and didn't see the muscle bunch at the edge of his jaw.

Would Nina be an invited guest? Dear Lord, she hoped not. Yet it was a possibility. A probability, she amended, aware that with each passing day the wedding drew closer. Which meant Nina would become more desperate to seize the slightest opportunity.

Aysha cursed beneath her breath at the thought of playing a part beneath Nina's watchful gaze. Worse, having to clash polite verbal swords with a woman whose vindictiveness was aimed to maim.

The harbour, with its various coves and inlets provided a scenic beauty unsurpassed anywhere in Australia, and she focused on the numerous small craft anchored at various moorings, cliff-top mansions dotted in between foliage.

Peak hour traffic had subsided, although it took the best part of an hour to reach their destination. A seemingly endless collection of long minutes when polite, meaningless conversation lapsed into silence.

'I guess our presence tonight is essential?'

Carlo cast her a direct look. 'If you're concerned Nina might be there...don't be. She won't have the opportunity to misbehave.'

'Do you really think you'll be able to stop her?' Aysha queried cynically.

He met her gaze for one full second, then returned his attention to the road. 'Watch me.'

'Oh, I intend to.' It could prove to be an interesting evening.

They reached the exclusive Palm Beach suburb at

the appointed time, and Aysha viewed the number of cars lining the driveway with interest. At a guess there were at least thirty guests.

Fifty, she re-calculated as their host drew them through the house and out onto the covered terrace.

It was strictly smile-time, and she was so well versed in playing the part that it was almost second nature to circulate among the guests and exchange small-talk.

A drink in one hand, she took a sip of excellent champagne and assured the hostess that almost every wedding detail was indeed organised, Claude, the wedding organiser, was indeed a gem, and, yes, she was desperately looking forward to the day.

Details she repeated many times during the next hour. She was still holding on to her first glass of champagne, and she took a hot savoury from a proffered platter, then reached for another.

'You missed dinner?'

Aysha spared Carlo a slow, sweet smile. 'How did you guess?'

His mouth curved, and his dark eyes held a musing gleam. 'You should have told me.'

'Why?'

The need to touch her was paramount, and he brushed fingertips down her cheek. 'We could have stopped somewhere for a meal.'

Her eyes flared, then dilated to resemble deep grey pools. 'Please don't.'

'Am I intruding on a little tiff?'

Aysha heard the words, recognised the feminine voice, and summoned a credible smile.

'Nina.'

Nina avidly examined Aysha's features, then fastened on the object of her obsession. She pressed exquisitely lacquered nails against the sleeve of Carlo's jacket. 'Trouble in paradise, *caro*?'

'What makes you think there might be?' His voice was pleasant, but there was no mistaking the icy hardness in his eyes as he removed Nina's hand from his arm.

Her pout was contrived to portray a sultry sexiness. 'Body language, darling.'

'Really?' The smile that curved his lips was a mere facsimile. 'In that case I would suggest your expertise is sadly lacking.'

Oh, my, Aysha applauded silently. If she could detach herself emotionally, the verbal parrying was shaping into an interesting bout.

'You know that isn't true.'

'Only by reputation. Not by personal experience.'

His voice was silk-encased steel, tempered to a dangerous edge. Only a fool would fail to recognise the folly of besting him.

'Darling, *really*. Your memory is so short?'

'We've frequented the same functions, sat at the same table. That's all.'

Nina spared Aysha a cursory glance. 'If you say so.' She gave a soft laugh and shook her head in telltale disbelief. 'The question is…will Aysha believe you?'

Aysha glimpsed the vindictive smile, registered the malevolence apparent in Nina's sweeping glance, before she turned back towards Carlo.

'*Ciao*, darlings. Have a happy life.'

Aysha watched Nina's sylph-like frame execute a deliberately evocative sway as she walked across the terrace.

'I think I need some fresh air.' And another glass of champagne. It might help dull the edges, and diminish the ugliness she'd just been witness to.

Strong fingers closed over her wrist. 'I'll come with you.'

'I'd rather go alone.'

'And add to Nina's satisfaction?'

Bright lights lit the garden paths, and there were guests mingling around the pool area. Music filtered through a speaker system, and there was the sound of muted laughter.

'Believe me, Nina's satisfaction is the last thing I want to think about.'

His grip on her hand tightened fractionally. 'I've never had occasion to lie to you, *cara*.' His eyes speared hers, fixing them mercilessly.

'There's always a first time for everything.'

Carlo was silent for several long seconds. 'I refuse to allow Nina's malicious machinations to destroy our relationship.'

The deadly softness of his voice should have warned her, but she was beyond analysing any nuances.

'Relationship?' Aysha challenged. 'Let's not delude ourselves our proposed union is anything other than a mutually beneficial business partnership.' She was on a roll, the words tripping easily, fatalistically, from her tongue. 'Cemented by holy matrimony in a bid to preserve a highly successful business empire for the next generation.' Her smile was far too bright, her voice so brittle she scarcely recognised it as her own.

Carlo's appraisal was swift, and she was totally unprepared as he lifted her slender frame over one shoulder.

An outraged gasp left her throat. 'What in *hell* do you think you're doing?'

'Taking you home.'

'Put me down.'

His silence was uncompromising, and she beat a fist against his ribcage in sheer frustration. With little effect, for he didn't release her until they reached the car.

'You *fiend*!' Aysha vented, uncaring of his ruthless expression as he unlocked the passenger door.

'Get in the car,' Carlo said hardily.

Her eyes sparked furiously alive. 'Don't you *dare* give me orders.'

He bit off a husky oath and pulled her in against him, then his head lowered and his mouth took punishing possession of her own.

Aysha struggled fruitlessly for several seconds, then whimpered as he held fast her head. His tongue was an invasive force, and she hated her traitorous body for the way it began to respond.

The hands which beat against each shoulder stilled and crept to link together at his nape. Her mouth softened, and she leaned in to him, uncaring that only seconds before anger had been her sole emotion.

She sensed the slight shudder that ran through his

large body, felt the hardening of his desire, and experienced the magnetising pulse of hunger in response.

Aysha felt as if she was drowning, and she temporarily lost any sense of time or where they were until Carlo gradually loosened his hold.

His lips trailed to the sensitive hollow at the edge of her neck and caressed it gently, then he lifted his head and bestowed a light, lingering kiss to her softly swollen mouth.

Sensation spiralled through her body, aching, poignant, making her aware of every nerve-centre, each pleasure spot.

Aysha didn't feel capable of doing anything but subsiding into the car, and she stared sightlessly out of the window as Carlo crossed to the driver's side and slid in behind the wheel.

She didn't offer a word for much of the time it took to reach Clontarf, for what could she say that wouldn't seem superfluous? The few occasions Carlo broached a query, her answer was monosyllabic.

Nina's image rose like a spectre in her mind, just as her voice echoed as the words replayed again and again.

CHAPTER NINE

THE Mercedes pulled off the main street and eased into a parking space. Carlo switched off the engine and undid his seatbelt.

Aysha looked at him askance. 'Why have you stopped?'

He reached sideways and unclasped her seatbelt. 'You didn't eat dinner, remember?'

The thought of food made her feel ill. 'I don't feel hungry.'

'Then we'll just have coffee.'

She looked at him in exasperation, and met the firm resolve apparent in his stance, the angle of his jaw.

'Do I get to have any say in this? Or will you employ strong-arm tactics?'

'You've dropped an essential kilo or two, you're pale, and you have dark circles beneath your eyes.'

'And I thought I was doing just fine,' Aysha declared silkily.

'It's here, or we raid the kitchen fridge at home.'

That meant him entering the house, making himself at home in the kitchen, and afterwards... She didn't want to contemplate *afterwards*. Having him stay was akin to condoning...

Oh, *damn*, she cursed wretchedly, and reached for the door-clasp.

The restaurant was well-patronised, and they were led to a centre table at the back of the room. Aysha heard the music, muted Mediterranean melancholy plucked from a boujouki, and the sound tugged something deep inside.

Carlo ordered coffee, and she declined. Greek coffee was ruinously strong.

'Tea. Very weak,' she added, and rolled her eyes when Carlo ordered moussaka from the menu. 'I don't want anything to eat.'

Moussaka was one of her favoured dishes, and when it arrived she spared it a lingering glance, let the aroma tease her nostrils. And she didn't argue when Carlo forked a portion and proffered a tempting sample.

It was delicious, and she picked up a spare fork and helped herself. Precisely as he'd anticipated she would do, she conceded wryly.

There was hot crusty bread, and she accepted a small glass of light red wine which she sipped throughout the meal.

'Better?'

It wasn't difficult to smile, and she could almost feel the relaxing effect of the wine releasing the knots of tension that curled tightly around her nerve-ends. 'Yes.'

'More tea?'

Aysha shook her head.

'Do you want to stay for a while, or shall we leave?'

She looked at him carefully, and was unable to define anything from his expression. There was a waiting, watchful quality apparent, a depth to his eyes that was impossible to interpret.

She spared a glance to the dance floor, and the few couples sharing it. Part of her wanted the contact, the closeness of his embrace. Yet there was another part that was truly torn.

Nina's accusations were too fresh in her mind, the image too vivid for it not to cloud her perspective.

Everything was wedding-related. And right now, the last thing she wanted to think about, let alone discuss, was the wedding.

'I adore the music. It's so poignant.'

Was she aware just how wistful she sounded? Or the degree of fragility she projected? Carlo wanted to smite a fist onto the table, or preferably close his hands around Nina's neck.

More than anything, he wanted to take Aysha to bed and make love with her until every last shred of doubt was removed. Yet he doubted she'd give him the opportunity. At least, not tonight.

Now, he had to be content to play the waiting game. Tomorrow, he assured himself grimly, he'd have everything he needed. And damned if he was going to wait another day.

He leaned across the table and caught hold of her hand, then lifted it to his lips.

It was an evocative gesture, and sent spirals of sensation radiating through her body. Her eyes dilated, and her lips shook slightly as he kissed each finger in turn.

'Dance with me.'

The shaking seemed to intensify, and she couldn't

believe it was evident. Dear God, dared she walk willingly into his arms?

And afterwards? What then? Let him lead her into the house, and into bed? That wouldn't resolve anything. Worse, the lack of a resolution would only condone her acquiescence to the status quo.

'Is dancing with me such a problem?' Carlo queried gently, and watched her eyes dilate to their fullest extent.

'It's what happens when I do.'

His eyes acquired a faint gleam, and the edges of his mouth tilted. 'Believe it's mutual.'

Aysha held his gaze without any difficulty at all. An hour ago she'd been furious with him. And Nina. *Especially* Nina.

'Pheromones,' she accorded sagely, and he uttered a soft laugh as he stood and drew her gently to her feet.

'The recognition by one animal of a chemical substance secreted by another,' Aysha informed him.

'You think so?'

She could feel her whole body begin to soften, from the inside out. A melting sensation that intensified as he brushed his lips against her temple.

'Yes.'

Would it always be like this? A smile, the touch of his mouth soothing the surface of her skin? *Is it enough*? a tiny voice taunted. Affection and sexual satisfaction, without love.

Many women settled for less. Much less.

He led her onto the dance floor and into his arms, and she didn't think about anything except the moment and the haunting, witching quality of the music as it stirred her senses and quickened the pace of her pulse.

Aysha wanted to close her eyes and think of nothing but the man and the moment.

For the space of a few minutes it was almost magic, then the music ceased as the band took a break, and she preceded Carlo back to the table.

'Another drink?'

'No, thanks,' she refused.

He picked up the account slip, summoned the waitress, paid, then led the way out to the car.

It didn't take long to reach Clontarf, and within minutes Carlo activated the gates, then drew the Mercedes to a halt outside the main entrance.

Aysha reached for the door-clasp as he released his seatbelt and opened the car door.

'There's no need—'

He shot her a glance that lost much of its intensity under cover of night. 'Don't argue,' he directed, and slid out from the car.

Indoors she turned to face him, and felt the sexual tension apparent. There was a slumberous quality in the depths of his eyes that curled all her nerve-ends, and she looked at him, assessing the leashed sensuality and matching it with her own.

'All you have to do is ask me to stay,' Carlo said quietly, and she looked at him with incredibly sad eyes.

It would be so easy. Just hold out her hand and follow wherever he chose to lead.

For a moment she almost wavered. To deny him

was to deny herself. Yet there were words she needed to say, and she wasn't sure she could make them sound right.

'I know.'

He lifted a hand and brushed his knuckles gently across her cheekbone. 'Go to bed, *cara*. Tomorrow is another day.'

Then he released her hand and turned towards the door.

Seconds later she heard the refined purr of the engine, and saw the bright red tail-lights disappear into the night.

He'd gone, when she'd expected him to employ unfair persuasion to share her bed. There was an ache deep inside she refused to acknowledge as disappointment.

If he'd pressed to stay, she'd have told him to leave. So why did she feel cheated?

Oh, for heaven's sake, this was ridiculous!

With a mental shake she locked the door and activated security, then she set the alarm and climbed the stairs to her room.

'Mamma,' Aysha protested. 'I don't *need* any more lingerie.'

'Nonsense, darling,' Teresa declared firmly. 'Nonna Benini sent money with specific instructions for you to buy lingerie.'

Aysha spared a glance at the exquisite bras, briefs and slips displayed in the exclusive lingerie boutique. Pure silk, French lace, and each costing enough money to feed an average family for a week.

After a sleepless night spent tossing and turning in her lonely bed, which had seen her wake with a headache, the last thing she needed was a confrontational argument with her mother.

'Then I guess we shouldn't disappoint her.'

Each garment had to be tried on for fit and size, and it was an hour before Aysha walked out of the boutique with bras and briefs in ivory, peach and black. Ditto slips, cobweb-fine pantyhose, and, the *pièce de resistance*, a matching nightgown and negligee.

'Superfluous,' she'd assured her mother when Teresa had insisted on the nightgown, and had stifled a sigh at her insistent glance.

Now, she tucked a hand beneath Teresa's arm and led her in the direction of the nearest café. 'Let's take five, Mamma, and share a cappuccino.'

'And we'll revise our list.'

Aysha thought if she heard the word *list* again, she'd scream. 'I can't think of a single thing.'

'Perfume. Something really special,' Teresa enthused. 'To wear on the day.'

'I already have—'

'I know. And it suits you so well.'

They entered the café, ordered, then chose a table near the window.

'But you should wear something subtly different, that you'll always associate with the most wonderful day of your life.'

'Mamma,' she protested, and was stalled in any further attempt as Teresa caught hold of her hands.

'A mother dreams of her child's wedding day from

the moment she gives birth. Especially a daughter. I want yours to be perfect, as perfect as it can be in every way.' Her eyes shimmered, and Aysha witnessed her conscious effort to control her emotions. 'With Carlo you'll have a wonderful life, enjoying the love you share together.'

A one-sided love, Aysha corrected silently. Many a successful marriage had been built on less. Was she foolish to wish for more? To want to be secure in the knowledge that Carlo had eyes only for her? That *she* was the only one he wanted, and no one else would do?

Chasing rainbows could be dangerous. If you did catch hold of one, there was no guarantee of finding the elusive pot of gold.

'Your father and I had a small wedding by choice,' Teresa continued. 'Our parents offered us money to use however we chose, and it was more important to use it towards the business.'

Aysha squeezed her mother's hand. 'I know, Mamma. I appreciate everything you've done for me.' Their love for each other wasn't in question, although she'd give almost anything to be able to break through the parent-child barrier and have Teresa be her friend, her equal.

However, Teresa was steeped in a different tradition, and the best she could hope for was that one day the balance of scales would become more even.

It was after eleven when they emerged into the arcade. Inevitably, Teresa's list had been updated to include perfume and a complete range of cosmetics and toiletries.

Aysha simply went with the flow, picked at a chicken salad when they paused for lunch, took two painkillers for her headache, and tried to evince interest in Teresa's summary of the wedding gifts which were beginning to arrive at her parents' home.

At three her mobile phone rang, and when she answered she heard Carlo's deep drawl at the other end of the line.

'Good day?'

Her heart moved up a beat. 'We're just about done.'

'I'll be at the house around seven.'

She was conscious of Teresa's interest, and she contrived to inject her tone with necessary warmth. 'Shall I cook something?'

'No, we'll eat out.'

'OK. *Ciao*.' She cut the connection and replaced the unit into her bag.

'Carlo,' Teresa deduced correctly, and Aysha inclined her head. 'He's a good man. You're very fortunate.'

There was only one answer she could give. 'I know.'

It was almost five when they parted, slipped into separate cars, and entered the busy stream of traffic, making it easy for Aysha to hang back at an intersection, then diverge onto a different road artery.

If Teresa discovered her daughter and prospective son-in-law were temporarily occupying separate residences, it would only arouse an entire host of questions Aysha had no inclination to answer.

The house was quiet, and she made her way upstairs, deposited a collection of brightly-coloured carry-bags in the bedroom, then discarded her clothes, donned a bikini and retraced her steps to the lower floor.

The pool looked inviting, and she angled her arms and dived into its cool depths, emerging to the surface to stroke several lengths before turning onto her back and lazily drifting.

Long minutes later she executed sufficient backstrokes to bring her to the pool's edge, then she levered herself onto the ledge and caught up a towel. Standing to her feet, she blotted excess moisture from her body, then she crossed to a nearby lounger and sank back against its cushioned depth.

The view out over the harbour was sheer magic, for at this hour the sea was a dark blue, deepening almost to indigo as it merged in the distance with the ocean.

There were three huge tankers drawing close to the main harbour entrance, and in the immediate periphery of her vision hundreds of small craft lay anchored at moorings.

It was a peaceful scene, and she closed her eyes against the strength of the sun's warmth. It had a soporific effect, and she could feel herself drifting into a light doze.

It was there that Carlo found her more than an hour later, after several minutes of increasing anxiety when he'd failed to locate her anywhere indoors.

His relief at seeing her lying supine on the lounger was palpable, although he could have shaken her for putting him through a few minutes of hell.

He slid open the door quietly, and stood watching her sleep. She looked so relaxed it was almost a shame to have to wake her, and he waited a while, not willing to disturb the moment.

A soft smile curved his mouth. He wanted to cross to her side and gently tease her into wakefulness. Lightly trail his fingers over the length of her body, brush his lips to her cheek, then find her mouth with his own. See her eyelids flutter then lift in wakefulness, and watch the warmth flood her eyes as she reached for him.

Except as things stood, the moment her lashes swept open her eyes were unlikely to reflect the emotion he wanted.

CHAPTER TEN

'AYSHA.'

She was dreaming, and she fought her way through the mists of sleep at the sound of her name.

The scene merged into reality. The location was right, so was the man who stood within touching distance.

It was the circumstances that were wrong.

She moved fluidly into a sitting position. 'Is it that late?' She swung her legs onto the ground and rose to her feet.

He looked impressive dressed in tailored trousers, pale blue cotton shirt, tie and jacket. She kept her eyes fixed on the knot of his tie. 'I'll go shower and change.'

He let her go, then followed her into the house. He crossed to the kitchen, extracted a cool drink from the refrigerator and popped the can, then he prowled around the large entertainment area, too restless to stand or sit in one place for long.

There were added touches he hadn't noticed before. Extra cushions on the chairs and sofas, prints hanging on the walls. The lines were clean and muted, but the room had a comfortable feeling; it was a place where it would be possible to relax.

Carlo checked his watch, and saw that only five minutes had passed. It would take her at least another thirty to wash and dry her hair, dress and apply make-up.

Forty-five, he accorded when she re-entered the room.

The slip dress in soft shell-pink with a chiffon overlay and a wide lace border on the hemline heightened her lightly tanned skin, emphasised her dark blonde hair, and clever use of mascara and shadow deepened the smoky grey of her eyes.

She'd twisted her hair into a knot atop her head, and teased free a tendril that curled down to the edge of her jaw.

Aysha found it easy to return his gaze with a level one of her own. Not so easy was the ability to slow the sudden hammering of her heart as she drew close.

'Shall we leave?' Her voice was even, composed, and at total variance to the rapid beat of her pulse.

'Before we do, there's something I want you to read.' Carlo reached for the flat manila envelope resting on the nearby table and handed it to her.

The warm and wonderful girl of a week ago no longer existed. Except in an acted portrayal in the presence of others.

Alone, the spontaneity was missing from her laughter, and her eyes were solemn in their regard. Absent too was the generous warmth in her smile.

The scene he'd initiated with Nina earlier in the day had been damaging, but he didn't give a damn. The woman's eagerness to accept his invitation to lunch had sickened him, and he hadn't wasted any time informing her exactly what he planned to do should she ever cause Aysha a moment's concern.

He'd gone to extraordinary lengths in an attempt to remove Aysha's doubts. Now he needed to tell her, *show* her.

'Read it, Aysha.'

'Can't it wait until later?'

He thrust a hand into a trouser pocket, and felt the tension twist inside his gut. 'No.'

There was a compelling quality evident in those dark eyes, and she glimpsed the tense muscle at the edge of his jaw.

She was familiar with every one of his features. The broad cheekbones, the crease that slashed each cheek, the wide-spaced large eyes that could melt her bones from just a glance. His mouth with its sensually moulded lips was to die for, and the firm jawline hinted at more than just strength of character.

'Please. Just read it.'

Aysha turned the envelope over, and her fingers sought the flap, dealt with it, then slid out the contents.

The first was a single page, sworn and signed with a name she didn't recognise. Identification of the witness required no qualification, for Samuel Sloane's prominence among the city's legal fraternity was legend.

Her eyes skimmed the print, then steadied into a slower pace as she took in the sworn affidavit testifying Nina di Salvo had engaged the photographic services of William Baker with specific instructions to capture Carlo Santangelo and herself in compromising positions, previously discussed and outlined, for the agreed sum of five hundred dollars per negative.

Aysha mentally added up the photographic prints Nina had shown her, and had her own suspicions confirmed. Carlo had been the target; Nina the arrow.

Her eyes swept up to meet his. 'I didn't think she'd go to these lengths.'

Carlo's eyes hardened as he thought of Nina's vitriolic behaviour. 'It's doubtful she'll bother either of us again.' He'd personally seen to it.

'Damage control,' Aysha declared, and saw his eyes darken with latent anger.

'Yes.'

It was remarkable how a single word could have more impact than a dozen or so. 'I see.'

She was beginning to. But there was still a way to go. 'Read the second document.'

Aysha carefully slipped the affidavit to one side. There were several pages, each one scripted in legalese phrased to confuse rather than clarify. However, there was no doubt of Carlo's instruction.

Any assets in whatever form, inherited from either parents' estates, were to remain solely in her name for her sole use. At such future time, Carlo Santangelo would assume financial responsibility for Benini-Santangelo.

There was only one question. 'Why?'

'Because I love you.'

Aysha heard the words, and her whole body froze. The stillness in the room seemed to magnify until it became a tangible entity.

Somehow she managed to dredge up her voice,

only to have it emerge as a sibilant whisper. 'If this is a trick, you can turn around and walk out of here.'

Her eyes became stricken with an emotion she couldn't hide, and his expression softened to something she would willingly give her life for.

He caught both her hands together with one hand, then lifted the other to capture her nape.

'I love you. *Love*,' he emphasised emotively. 'The heart and soul that is *you*.' He moved his thumb against the edge of her jaw, then slowly swept it up to encompass her cheekbone. His eyes deepened, and his voice lowered to an impassioned murmur. 'I thought the love Bianca and I shared was irreplaceable. But I was wrong.' He lowered his forehead down to rest against hers. 'There was you. Always you. Affection, from the moment you were born. Respect, as you grew from child to woman. Admiration, for carving out your own future.'

His hands moved to her shoulders, then curved down her back to pull her close in against him.

It would be all too easy to lean in and lift her mouth to meet his. As she had in the past. This time she wanted sanity unclouded by emotion or passion.

Aysha lifted her hands to his chest and tried to put some distance between them. Without success. 'I can't think when you hold me.'

Those dark eyes above her own were so deeply expressive, she thought she might drown in them.

'Is it so important that you think?' he queried gently, and she swallowed compulsively.

'Yes.' She was conscious of every breath she took, every beat of her heart.

Carlo let his hands drop, and his features took on a quizzical warmth.

What she wanted, she hardly dared hope for, and she looked at him in silence as the seconds ticked by.

His smile completely disarmed her, and warmth seeped into her veins, heating and gathering force until it ran through her body.

'You want it all, don't you?'

Her mouth trembled as she fought to control her emotions. She was shaking, inwardly. Very soon, she'd become a trembling mass. 'Yes.'

Carlo pushed both hands into his trouser pockets, and she was mesmerised by his mouth, the way it curved and showed the gleam of white teeth, the sensuous quirk she longed to touch.

'I knew marriage between us could work. We come from the same background, we move in the same social circles, and share many interests. We had the foundation of friendship and affection to build on.'

The vertical crease slashed each cheek as he smiled, and his eyes... She felt as if she could drown in their depths.

'In the beginning I was satisfied that it was enough. I didn't expect to have those emotions develop into something more, much more.'

She had to ask. 'And now?'

'I need to be part of your life, to have you need me as much as I need you. As my wife, my friend, the other half of my soul.' He released his hands and reached out to cup her face. 'To love you, as you deserve to be loved. With all my heart. For the rest of my life.'

Aysha felt the ache of tears, and blinked rapidly to dispel them. At that precise moment she was incapable of uttering a word.

Did she realise how transparent she was? Intimacy was a powerful weapon, persuasive, invasive, and one he could use with very little effort. It would be so easy to lower his head, pull her close and let her *feel* what she did to him. His hands soothing her body, the possession of his mouth on hers...

He did none of those things.

'Yes.'

He heard the single affirmative, and every muscle, every nerve relaxed. Nothing else mattered, except their love and the life they would share together. 'No qualifications?'

She shook her head. 'None.'

'So sure,' Carlo said huskily. He reached for her, enfolding her into the strength of his body as his mouth settled over hers. Gently at first, savouring, tasting, then with a passionate fervour as she lifted her arms and linked her hands together at his nape.

Aysha felt his body tremble as she absorbed the force of his kiss and met and matched the mating dance of his tongue as it explored and ravaged sensitive tissue.

His hands shaped and soothed as they sought each pleasure spot, stroking with infinite care as the fire ignited deep within and burst into flame.

It seemed an age before he lifted his head, and she

could only stand there, supported by the strength of his arms.

'Do you trust me?'

She heard the depth in his voice, sensed his seriousness, and raised her eyes to meet his. There was no question. 'Yes,' she said simply.

'Then let's go.'

'OK.'

'Such docility,' Carlo teased gently as he brushed his lips against one temple.

Aysha placed a hand either side of his head and tilted it down as she angled her mouth into his in a kiss that was all heat and passion.

His heart thudded into a quickened beat, and she felt a thrill of exhilaration at the sense of power, the feeling of control.

Carlo broke the contact with emotive reluctance. 'The temptation to love you now, *here*, is difficult to resist.'

A mischievous smile curved her mouth. 'But you're going to.'

His hands slid to her shoulders and he gave her a gentle shake. 'Believe it's merely a raincheck, *cara*.' He released her and took hold of her hand.

'Are you going to tell me *where* we're going?'

'Someplace special.'

He led her outside, then turned to the side path leading to the rear of the grounds.

'Here?' Aysha queried in puzzlement, as they traversed the short set of steps leading down to the gazebo adjacent the pool area.

Lights sprang to life as if by magic, illuminating

the gazebo and casting a reflected glow over the newly planted garden, the beautiful free-form pool.

Her eyes widened as she saw a man and two women standing in front of a small rectangular pedestal draped with a pristine white lace-edged cloth. Two thick candles displayed a thin flicker and a vaporous plume, and there was the scent of roses, beautiful white tight-petalled buds on slender stems.

'Carlo?'

Even as she voiced the query she saw the answer in those dark eyes, eloquent with emotive passion. And love.

'This is for us,' he said gently, curving an arm across the back of her waist as he pulled her into the curve of his body. 'Saturday's production will fulfil our parents' and the guests' expectations.'

She was melting inside, the warmth seeping through her body like molten wax, and she didn't know whether to laugh or cry.

An hour ago she'd been curled up on a soft-cushioned sofa contemplating her shredded emotions.

'OK?' Carlo queried gently.

Her heart kicked in at a quickened beat, and she smiled. A slow, sweet smile that mirrored her inner radiance. 'Yes.'

Introductions complete, Aysha solemnly took her position at Carlo's side.

If the celebrant was surprised at the bride and groom's attire, she gave no indication of it. Her manner appeared genuine, and the words she spoke held a wealth of meaning during the short service.

Carlo slipped a diamond-encrusted ring onto her

finger, and Aysha slid a curved gold band onto his, listening in a haze of emotions as they were solemnly pronounced man and wife.

She lifted her mouth to meet his, and felt the warmth, the hint of restrained passion as he savoured the sweetness and took his fill.

Oh, my, this was about as close to heaven as it was possible to get, Aysha conceded as he reluctantly loosened his hold.

The heat was there, evident in the depth of his eyes, banked down beneath the surface. Desire, and promised ecstasy.

She cast him a witching smile, glimpsed the hunger and felt anticipation arrow through her body.

There was champagne chilling in an ice bucket, and Carlo loosened the cork, then filled each flute with slightly frothy sparkling liquid.

The bubbles tingled her tastebuds and teased the back of her throat as she sipped the excellent vintage.

Each minute seemed like an eternity as she conversed with the celebrant and two witnesses, and accepted the toast.

With both official and social duties completed, the celebrant graciously took her leave, together with the couple who had witnessed the marriage.

Aysha stood in the circle of Carlo's arms, and she leaned back against him, treasuring the closeness, the sheer joy attached to the moment.

Married. She could hardly believe it. There were so many questions she needed to ask. But not yet. There would be time later to work out the answers.

For now, she wanted to savour the moment.

Carlo's lips teased her sensitive nape, then nuzzled an earlobe. 'You're very quiet.'

'I feel as if we're alone in the universe,' she said dreamily. Her mouth curved upwards. 'Well, almost.' A faint laugh husked low in her throat. 'If you block out the cityscape, the tracery of street lights, the suburban houses.'

'I thought by now you'd have unleashed a barrage of questions,' he said with quizzical amusement.

She felt the slide of his hand as he reached beneath her top and sought her breast. The familiar kick of sensation speared from her feminine core, and she groaned emotively as his skilled fingers worked magic with the delicate peak.

She turned in his arms and reached for him, pulling his head down to hers as she sought his mouth with her own in a kiss that wreaked havoc with her tenuous control.

Aysha was almost shaking when he gently disengaged her, and her lips felt faintly swollen, her senses completely swamped with the feel, the taste of him.

'Let's get out of here,' Carlo directed huskily as he caught hold of her hand and led her towards his car.

'Where are we going?'

'I've booked us into a hotel suite for the night. Dinner at the restaurant. Champagne.'

'Why?' she queried simply. 'When everything we need is right here?'

'I want the night to be memorable.'

'It will be.' Without a doubt, she promised silently.

'You don't want the luxurious suite, a leisurely meal with champagne?' he teased.

'I want *you*. Only you,' Aysha vowed with heart-felt sincerity. 'Saturday we get to go through the formalities.' The elegant bridal gown, the limousines, the church service, the extravagant reception, she mused silently. Followed by the hotel bridal suite, and the flight out the next morning to their honeymoon destination.

A bewitching smile curved her generous mouth, and her eyes sparkled with latent humour. 'Tonight we can please ourselves.'

Carlo pressed a light kiss to the edge of her lips. 'Starting now?'

'Here?' she countered wickedly. 'And shock the neighbours?'

He swept an arm beneath her knees and carried her into the house. He traversed the stairs without changing stride, and in the main bedroom he lowered her down to stand in front of him.

Slowly, with infinite care, he released her zip. Warm fingers slid each strap over her shoulders, then shaped the soft slip down over her hips, her thighs, to her feet. Only her briefs and bra remained, and he dispensed with those.

She ached for his touch, his possession, and she closed her eyes, then opened them again as he lightly brushed his fingers across her sensitised skin.

He followed each movement with his lips, each single touch becoming a torture until she reached for him, her fingers urgent as they released shirt buttons and tugged the expensive cotton from his muscular frame.

His eyes dilated as she undid the buckle of his belt, and he caught his breath as she worked the zip fastening.

'Not quite in control, huh?' she offered with a faintly wicked smile, only to gasp as his mouth sought a vulnerable hollow at the edge of her neck.

He had the touch, the skill to evoke an instant response, and she trembled as his tongue wrought renewed havoc.

His hands closed over hers, completing the task, and she clutched hold of his waist as he dispensed with the remainder of his clothes.

The scent of his skin, the slight muskiness of *man* intermingled with the elusive tones of soap and cologne. Tantalising, erotic, infinitely tempting, and inviting her to savour and taste.

Aysha felt sensation burgeon until it encompassed every nerve-cell. The depth, the magnitude overwhelmed her. Two souls melding, seamlessly forging a bond that could never be broken.

She lifted her arms and wound them round his neck as he lowered her down onto the bed and followed her, protecting her from the full impact of his weight.

His mouth closed over hers, devastatingly sensual, in a kiss that drugged her mind, her senses, until she hardly recognised the guttural pleas as her own.

She was on fire, the flames of desire burning deep within until there was no reason, no sensation of anything other than the man and the havoc he was causing as he led her through pleasure to ecstasy and beyond.

Now, she wanted him *now*. The feel of him inside her, surging again and again, deeper and deeper, until she absorbed all of him, and their rhythm became as one, in tune and in perfect accord as they soared together, clung momentarily to the sexual pinnacle, then reached the ultimate state of nirvana.

Did she say the words? She had no idea whether they found voice or not. There was only the journey, the sensation of spiralling ecstasy, the scent of sexual essence, and the damp sheen on his skin.

She was conscious of her own response, *his*, the shudder raking that large body as he spilled his seed, and she exulted in the moment.

The sex between them had always been good. Better than good, she accorded dimly as she clung to him. But this, this was more. Intoxicating, exquisite, wild. And there was *love*. That essential quality that transcended physical expertise or skill.

There was no contest, Aysha acknowledged with lazy warmth a long time later as she lay curled against a hard male body.

Neither had had the will to indulge in leisurely lovemaking the first time round. It had been hard and fast, each one of them *driven* by a primal urge so intense it had been electrifying, wanton, and totally impassioned.

Afterwards they had shared the Jacuzzi, then towelled dry, they'd returned to bed for a lingering aftermath of touching, tasting...a *loving* that had had no equal in anything they'd previously shared.

'Are we going to tell our parents?'

Carlo brushed his chin against the top of her head. 'Let a slight change in wording to *reaffirmation* of vows do it for us on the day.'

CHAPTER ELEVEN

AYSHA woke to the sound of rain, and she took a moment to stretch her limbs, then she checked the bedside clock. A few minutes past seven.

Any time soon Teresa would knock on her door, and the day would begin.

If she was fortunate, she had an hour, maybe two, before Teresa began checking on everything from the expected delivery time of flowers...to the house, the church, the reception. Followed by a litany of reminders that would initiate various supervisors to re-check arrangements with their minions. The wedding co-ordinator was doubtless on the verge of a nervous breakdown.

Aysha slid out from the bed and padded barefoot across the carpet to the draped window. A touch to the remote control module activated the mechanism that swept the drapes open, and she stifled a groan at the sight of heavy rain drenching the lawn.

Her mother, she knew, would consider it an omen, and probably not a propitious one.

Aysha selected shorts and a top, discarded her nightshirt, then quickly dressed. With a bit of celestial help she might make it downstairs to the dining room—

Her mobile phone rang, and she reached for it.

'Carlo?'

'Who else were you expecting?'

His deep voice did strange things to her senses, and the temptation to tease him a little was difficult to resist. 'Any one of my four bridesmaids, your mother, Nonna Benini, phoning from Treviso to wish me *buona fortuna*, Sister Maria Teresa...' she trailed off, and was unable to suppress a light laugh. 'Is there any particular reason you called?'

'Remind me to exact retribution, *cara*,' he mocked in husky promise.

The thought of precisely how he would achieve it curled round her central core, and set her heart beating at a quickened pace.

'You weren't there when I reached out in the night,' Carlo said gently. 'There was no scent of you on my sheets, no drift of perfume to lend assurance to my subconscious mind.' He paused for a few seconds. 'I missed you.'

She closed her eyes against the vivid picture his words evoked. She could feel her whole body begin to heat, her emotions separate and shred. 'Don't,' she pleaded with a slight groan. 'I have to get through the day.'

'Didn't sleep much, either, huh?' he queried wryly, and she wrinkled her nose.

'An hour or two, here and there,' Aysha admitted.

'Are you dressed?'

'Yes.' Her voice was almost prim, and he laughed.

'Pity. If I can't have you in the flesh, then the fantasy will have to suffice.'

'And you, of course, have had a workout, showered, shaved, and are about to eat breakfast?'

Carlo chuckled, a deep, throaty sound that sent shivers slithering down her spine. 'Actually, no. I'm lying in bed, conserving my energy.'

Just the thought of that long muscular body resting supine on the bed was enough to play havoc with her senses. Imagining how he might or might not be attired sent her pulse beating like a drum.

'I don't think we'd better do this.'

'Do *what*, precisely?'

'Phone sex.'

His voice held latent laughter. 'Is that what you think we're doing?'

'It doesn't compensate for the real thing.'

His soft laughter was almost her undoing. 'I doubt Teresa will be impressed if I appear at the door and sweep you into the bedroom before breakfast.'

A firm tattoo sounded against the panelled door. 'Aysha?'

The day was about to start in earnest. 'In a moment, Mamma.'

'Don't keep me waiting too long at the church, *cara*,' Carlo said gently as she crossed the room.

'To be five minutes late is obligatory,' she teased, twisting the knob and drawing back the door. *'Ciao.'*

Teresa stood framed in the doorway. *'Buon giorno*, darling.' Her eyes glanced at the mobile phone. 'You were talking to Carlo?' She didn't wait for an answer as she walked to the expanse of plate glass window with its splendid view of the harbour and northern suburbs. 'It's raining.'

'The service isn't scheduled until four,' Aysha attempted to soothe.

'Antonio has spent so much time and effort on the gardens these past few weeks. It will be such a shame if we can't assemble outside for photographs.'

'The wedding organiser has a contingency plan, Mamma.' Photographs in the conservatory, the massive entry foyer, the lounge.

'Yes, I know. But the garden would be perfect.'

Aysha sighed. The problem with a perfectionist was that rarely did *anything* meet their impossibly high expectations.

'Mamma,' she began gently. 'If it's going to rain, it will, and worrying won't make it different.' She crossed to the *en suite* bathroom. 'Give me a few minutes, then we'll go downstairs and share breakfast.'

It was the antithesis of a leisurely meal. The phone rang constantly, and at nine the first of the day's wedding gifts arrived by delivery van.

'Put them in here,' Teresa instructed, leading the way into a sitting room where a long table decorated with snowy white linen and draped tulle held a large collection of various sized wrapped and beribboned packages.

The doorchimes sounded. 'Aysha, get that, will you, darling? It'll probably be Natalina or Giovanna.'

The first in line of several friends who had offered their services to help.

'Aysha, you look so calm. How is that?'

Because Carlo loves me. And we're already married. The words didn't find voice, but they sang through her brain like the sweetest music she'd ever heard.

'Ask me again a few hours from now,' she said with a teasing smile.

Organisation was the key, although as the morning progressed the order changed to relative chaos and went downhill from there.

The florist delivered the bridal bouquets, exquisitely laid out in their boxes…except there was one missing. The men's buttonholes arrived with the bouquets, instead of being delivered to Gianna's home.

Soon after that problem was satisfactorily resolved Teresa received a phone call from one of the two women who'd offered to decorate the church pews…they couldn't get in, the church doors were locked, and no one appeared to be answering their summons.

Lunch was hardly an issue as time suddenly appeared to be of the essence, with the arrival of Lianna, Arianne, Suzanne and Tessa.

'*Très* chic, darling,' Lianna teased as she appraised Aysha from head to toe and back again. 'Bare feet, cut-off jeans and a skimpy top. The ultimate in avant-garde bridal wear. Just add the veil, and you'll cause a sensation,' she concluded with droll humour.

'Mamma would have a heart attack.'

'Not something to be countenanced,' Lianna agreed solemnly. 'Now,' she demanded breezily, 'we're all showered and ready to roll. Command, and we'll obey.'

Together they went over the *modus operandi*, which went a little haywire, as the hairdresser arrived early and the make-up artist was late.

There followed a lull of harmonious activity until

it became volubly clear Giuseppe was insistent on wearing navy socks instead of black, and an argument ensued, the pitch of frazzled voices rising when Teresa laddered new tights.

'Ah, your *mamma…*' Giuseppe sighed eloquently as he entered the dining room where the hairdresser was putting the finishing touches to Aysha's hair.

'I love you, Papà,' Aysha said softly, and saw his features dissolve into gentleness.

'Grazie.' His eyes moistened, and he blinked rapidly. 'The photographer, he will be here soon. Better you go upstairs and get into that dress, or we'll both have your Mamma to answer to, hmm.'

She gave him a quick hug, touched her fingers to his cheek, and smiled as he caught hold of them and bestowed a kiss to her palm. 'A father couldn't wish for a more beautiful daughter. Now go.'

When she reached her bedroom Teresa was fussing over the bridesmaids' gowns in a bid to ensure every detail was perfect.

Lianna rolled her eyes in silent commiseration, then exhibited the picture of genteel grace. 'When are the little terrors due to arrive?'

'My God,' Teresa cried with pious disregard as she swept to face Aysha. 'The rose petals. Did you see a plastic container of rose petals in the florist's box?'

Aysha shook her head, and Teresa turned and all but ran from the room.

'For heaven's sake, darling,' Lianna encouraged. 'Get into that fairy floss of a dress, we'll zip you up, stick on the headpiece and veil—' An anguished wail rent the air. 'Guess the rose petals were a no-show, huh?' she continued conversationally. 'I'll go offer my assistance before dear Teresa adds a nervous breakdown to the imminent heart attack.'

Ten minutes later she was back, and Aysha merely lifted one eyebrow in silent query.

'One container of rose petals found safe and sound at Gianna's home. As we need *two*, Giuseppe has been despatched to denude Antonio's precious rose bushes.'

'Whose idea was that?' Aysha shook her head in a silent gesture of mock despair. 'Don't tell me. Yours, right?'

Lianna executed a sweeping bow. 'Of course. What the hell else were we going to do?' She inclined her head, then gave a visible shudder. 'Here come the cavalry of infants.'

Aysha removed her wedding dress from its hanger, then with the girls' help she carefully stepped into it and eased it gently into place. The zip slid home, and she adjusted the scalloped lace at her wrist.

The fitted bodice with its overlay of lace was decorated with tiny seed pearls, and the scooped neckline displayed her shoulders to perfection. A full-length skirt flowed in a cluster of finely gathered pleats from her slender waist and fell in a cascade of lace. The veil was the finest tulle, edged with filigree lace and held in place by an exquisite head piece fashioned from seed pearls and tiny silk flowers.

'Wow,' Lianna, Arianne, Suzanne and Tessa accorded with reverence as she turned to face them, and Lianna, inevitably the first to speak, declared, 'You're a princess, sweetheart. A real princess.'

Lianna held out her hand, and, in the manner of a surgeon requesting instruments, she demanded, 'Shoes? Garter in place? Head piece and veil.' That took several minutes to fix. 'Something borrowed?' She tucked a white lace handkerchief into Aysha's hand. 'Something blue?' A cute bow tucked into the garter. 'Something old?'

Aysha touched the diamond pendant on its thin gold chain.

Teresa re-entered the room and came to an abrupt halt. 'The children are waiting downstairs with the photographer.' Her voice acquired a betraying huskiness. '*Dio Madonna*, I think I'm going to cry.'

'No, you're not. Think of the make-up,' Lianna cajoled. 'Then we'd have to do it over, which would make us late.' She made a comical face. 'The mother of the bride gets to cry *after* the wedding.' She patted Teresa's shoulder with theatrical emphasis. 'Now's the time you launch yourself into your daughter's arms, assure her she's the most beautiful girl ever born, and any other mushy stuff you want to add. Then,' she declared with considerable feeling, 'we smile prettily while the photographer does his thing, and get the princess here to the church on time.'

Teresa's smile was shaky, definitely shaky, as she crossed to Aysha and placed a careful kiss on first one cheek, then the other. 'It's just beautiful.' She swallowed quickly. 'You're beautiful. Oh, dear—'

'Whoa,' Lianna cautioned. 'Time to go.'

The photographer took almost an hour, utilising indoor shots during a drizzling shower. Then miraculously the sun came out as they took their seats in no fewer than three stretch limousines parked in line on the driveway.

'Well, Papà, this is it,' Aysha said softly. 'We're on our way.'

He reached out and patted her hand. 'You'll be happy with Carlo.'

'I know.'

'Did I tell you how beautiful you look?'

Aysha's eyes twinkled with latent humour. 'Mamma chose well, didn't she?'

His answering smile held a degree of philosophical acceptance. 'She has planned this day since you were a little girl.'

The procession was slow and smooth as the cavalcade of limousines descended the New South Head Road.

Stately, Aysha accorded silently as the first of the cars slowed and turned into the church grounds.

There were several guests waiting outside, and there was the flash of cameras as Giuseppe helped her out from the rear seat.

Lianna and Arianne checked the hem of her gown, smoothed the veil, then together they made their way to the church entrance, where Suzanne and Tessa were schooling the children into position.

The entire effect came together as a whole, and Aysha took a moment to admire her bridal party.

Each of the bridesmaids wore burgundy silk off-the-shoulder fitted gowns and carried bouquets of ivory orchids. The flower girls wore ivory silk full-length dresses with puffed sleeves and a wide waist-band, tied at the back in a large bow, with white shoes completing their attire, while the two page boys each wore a dark suit, white shirt with a paisley silk waistcoat and black bow-tie.

Teresa arrived, and Aysha watched as her mother distributed both satin ring cushions and supervised the little girls with their baskets of rose petals.

This was as much Teresa's day as it was hers, and she smiled as she took Giuseppe's arm. 'Ready, Papà?'

He was giving her into the care of another man, and it meant much to him, Aysha knew, that Carlo met with his full approval.

The organ changed tempo and began the 'Bridal March' as they entered the church, and Aysha saw Carlo standing at the front edge of the aisle, flanked by his best man and groomsmen.

Emily and Samantha strewed rose petals on the carpet in co-ordinated perfection. Neither Jonathon nor Gerard dropped the ring cushions.

As she walked towards Carlo he flouted convention and turned to face her. She saw the glimpse of fierce pride mingling with admiration, love meshing with adoration. Then he smiled. For her, only for her.

Everything else faded to the periphery of her vision, for she saw only him, and her smile matched his own as she moved forward and stood at his side.

Carlo reached for her hand and covered it with his own as the priest began the ceremony.

The substitution *reaffirmation* of their vows seemed to take on an electric significance as the guests assimilated the change of words.

Renewed pledges, the exchange of rings, and the

long, passionate kiss that undoubtedly would become a topic of conversation at many a dinner table for months to come.

There was music, not the usual hymn, but a poignant song whose lyrics brought a lump to many a guest's throat. A few feminine tears brought the use of fine cotton handkerchiefs when the groom leaned forward and gently kissed his bride for the second time.

Then Aysha took Carlo's arm and walked out of the church and into the sunshine to face a barrage of photographers.

It was Lianna who organised the children and cajoled them to behave with decorum during the photographic shoot. Aysha hid a smile at the thought they were probably so intimidated they didn't think to do anything but obey.

'She's going to drive some poor man mad,' Carlo declared with a musing smile, and Aysha laughed, a low, sparkling sound that was reflected in the depths of her eyes.

'And he'll adore every minute of it,' she predicted.

The shift to the reception venue was achieved on schedule, and Aysha turned to look at Carlo as their limousine travelled the short distance from the church.

'You were right,' she said quietly. 'I wouldn't have missed the church service for the world.'

His smile melted her bones, and her stomach executed a series of crazy somersaults as he took her hands to his lips and kissed each one in turn.

'I'll carry the image of you walking towards me down the aisle for the rest of my life.'

She traced a gentle finger down the vertical crease of his cheek and lingered at the edge of his mouth. 'Now we get to cut the cake and drink champagne.'

'And I get to dance with my wife.'

'Yes,' she teased mercilessly. 'After the speeches, the food, the photographs...'

'Then I get to take you home.'

Oh, my. She breathed unsteadily. How was she going to get through the next few hours?

With the greatest of ease, she reflected several hours later as they circled the guests and made their farewells.

Teresa deserved tremendous credit, for without doubt she had staged the production of her dreams and turned it into the wedding of the year. Press coverage, the media, the church, ceremony, catering, cake... Everything had gone according to plan, except for a few minor hiccups.

A very special day, and one Aysha would always treasure. But it was the evening she and Carlo had exchanged their wedding vows that would remain with her for the rest of her life.

Saying goodbye to her parents proved an emotional experience, for among their happiness and joy she could sense a degree of sadness at her transition from daughter to wife.

Tradition died hard, and Aysha hugged them tight and conveyed her appreciation not only for the day and the night, but for the care and devotion they'd accorded her from the day she was born.

There was confetti, rice, and much laughter as they escaped to the limousine. A short drive to an inner city hotel, and then the ascent by lift to the suite Carlo had booked for the night.

Aysha gave a startled gasp as he released the door then swept her into his arms and carried her inside.

'Now,' he began teasingly, as he pulled her close. 'I get to do this.'

This was a very long, intensely passionate kiss, and she just held on and clung as she met and matched his raw, primitive desire.

Then he gently released her and crossed to the table, where champagne rested on ice.

Aysha watched as Carlo loosened the cork on the bottle of champagne.

Froth spilled from the neck in a gentle spume, and she laughed softly as he picked up a flute to catch the foaming liquid.

'I've done that successfully at least a hundred times.' He partly filled another, then he handed her one, and touched the rim with his own. 'To us.'

Her mouth curved to form a generous smile, and her eyes... A man could drown in those luminous grey depths, at times mysterious, winsome, wicked. Today they sparkled with warmth, laughter and love. He wanted to reach out and pull her into his arms. Hold and absorb her until she was part of him, and never let go.

'Happiness, always,' said Aysha gently, and sipped the fine champagne.

He placed the bottle and the flute down onto the

coffee table, then he gently cradled her face between both hands.

'I love you.' His mouth closed over hers in a soft, open-mouthed kiss which reduced her to a quivering boneless mass.

'Have I told you how beautiful you looked today?' Carlo queried long minutes later.

After three times she'd stopped counting. 'Yes,' she teased, pressing a finger against the centre of his lower lip. Her eyes dilated as he took the tip into his mouth and began to caress it slowly with his tongue.

Heat suffused her veins, coursing through her body until she was on fire with need.

'There's just one thing.'

He buried his mouth in its palm. 'Anything.'

'Fool,' she accorded gently, and watched in fascination as his expression assumed a seriousness that was at variance with the day, the hour, the moment.

'Anything, *cara*,' he repeated solemnly. 'Any time, anywhere. All you have to do is ask.'

She closed her eyes, then slowly opened them. It frightened her to think she had so much power over this man. It was a quality she intended to treat with the utmost respect and care.

'I have something for you.'

'I don't need anything,' Carlo assured her. 'Except *you*.'

She kissed him briefly. 'I'm not going anywhere.' What she sought reposed within easy reach, and she took the few steps necessary to extract the white envelope, then she turned and placed it in his hand.

'*Cara*? What is this?'

A telephone call, specific instructions, a lecture on the necessity to protect her interests, and time out in a very hectic schedule to attach her signature in the presence of her legal advisor.

'Open and read it.'

Carlo's eyes sharpened as he extracted the neatly pinned papers, and as he unfolded and began to scan the affidavit it became apparent what she'd done.

He lowered the papers and regarded her carefully. 'Aysha—'

'I love you. I always have, for as long as I can remember.' She thought she might die from the intensity of it. 'I always will.'

It was a gift beyond price. 'I know.' Carlo's voice was incredibly gentle. Just as his love for her would endure. It was something he intended to reinforce every day for the rest of his life.

'Come here,' he bade softly, extending his arms, and she went into them gladly, wrapping her own round his waist as he enfolded her close.

The papers fluttered to the floor as his lips covered hers, and she gave herself up to the sensual magic that was theirs alone.

Heaven didn't get much better than this, Aysha mused dreamily as he swept an arm beneath her knees and strode towards the stairs.

'*Ti amo*,' she whispered. '*Ti amo.*'

Carlo paused and took possession of her mouth with his own in a kiss that held so much promise she almost wept. '*In eterno.*' Eternity, and beyond.

London's streets aren't just paved with gold—they're home to three of the world's most eligible bachelors!

You can meet these gorgeous men, and the women who steal their hearts, in:

NOTTING HILL GROOMS

Look out for these tantalizing romances set in London's exclusive Notting Hill, written by highly acclaimed authors who, between them, have sold more than 35 million books worldwide!

Irresistible Temptation by Sara Craven
Harlequin Presents® #2077
On sale December 1999

Reform of the Playboy by Mary Lyons
Harlequin Presents® #2083
On sale January 2000

The Millionaire Affair by Sophie Weston
Harlequin Presents® #2089
On sale February 2000

Available wherever Harlequin books are sold.

HARLEQUIN®
Makes any time special™

HARLEQUIN PRESENTS®

Seduction
SWEET REVENGE

They wanted to get even.
Instead they got...married!
by bestselling author
Penny Jordan

Don't miss Penny Jordan's latest enthralling miniseries
about four special women. Kelly, Anna, Beth and Dee
share a bond of friendship and a burning desire to
avenge a wrong. But in their quest for revenge, they
each discover an even stronger emotion.
Love.

Look out for all four books in Harlequin Presents®:

November 1999
THE MISTRESS ASSIGNMENT

December 1999
LOVER BY DECEPTION

January 2000
A TREACHEROUS SEDUCTION

February 2000
THE MARRIAGE RESOLUTION

Available at your favorite retail outlet.

HARLEQUIN®
Makes any time special ™

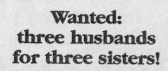

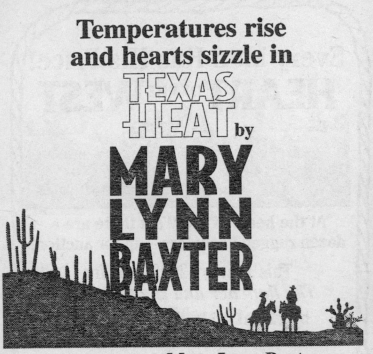

HARLEQUIN PRESENTS®

EXPECTING!

She's sexy, she's successful... and she's pregnant!

Relax and enjoy these new stories about spirited women and gorgeous men, whose passion results in pregnancies... sometimes unexpectedly! All the new parents-to-be will discover that the business of making babies brings with it the most special love of all....

Available wherever Harlequin books are sold.

HARLEQUIN®
Makes any time special ™

Look us up on-line at: http://www.romance.net

HPEXP4